ALL THE YAGE IN RENO

by

Robert Rahula

ALSO BY ROBERT RAHULA

NOVELS:
Messieurs
Panamaniac
Island of Misfits
Day Another Paradise In
One Last Fling
Bathhouse Stories
Conversation in a Belgian Bar
Exigent Circumstances
Uninvited Guest

POETRY:
Trigger Points
Dentro Del Corazón Bloqueada
Camino
Migration
I Sing the Body Politic
Wonderland
From Whose Bourn
Poemas Españoles
Expat Poems

SHORT STORIES:
Horror Stories for Children

ANTHOLOGIES:
Half Life
The Essential Dan Landes

ALL THE YAGE IN RENO

First Printing 2018
ISBN *978-0-9994736-5-8*

Alma-gator Press

Barcelona • Madrid • La Chorrera

There are more things in heaven and earth, Horatio,
Than are dreamt of in your philosophy.

—Hamlet, Act 1, Scene 5.

Chapter 1

Reno was not where Dan wanted to end up. It was a crappy town, as dirty and worn-out as the bums and homeless on its street corners, long past its prime as the Silver City of the West, surviving solely on the life-support of the casino convention business. The weekend gamblers and wannabe high rollers from northern California had stopped coming to Reno decades ago, when a wall of more convenient casinos sprung up like mushrooms in a long line growing vertically down northeastern California. Any road to Reno that a gambler could take from Napa, San Francisco, Sacramento, or San Jose would pass half a dozen casinos before the driver even got to the Nevada state line, so why bother? Every time a new casino opened in northern California, Reno felt its revenues drop another notch. The city of Reno depended on its casinos to survive, so the city fathers and the casino owners met together and came up with a joint plan to develop the convention business. They didn't have a choice. It was the only delivery system of gamblers left open to them. The casinos did everything they could to solicit the conventions and conferences, because it was the only way to funnel customers into the casinos; and conventioneers, union members, and agency workers all over the Western United States urged their bosses to schedule annual meetings in Reno so they could slip away from the meetings to visit the legal brothels in Sparks without raising the suspicions of their wives. The Reno city fathers did their part by secretly lobbying to protect the legalized prostitution in neighboring Sparks. And why not? The brothels around Sparks were a less than a twenty-minute cab ride away—convenient for conventioneers but just far enough away that Reno could claim clean hands. It was the perfect arrangement, as symbiotic as any intestinal parasite: The casinos kept the convention space rentals low—often times running them at a loss—in order to generate players for the slot machines, the craps tables, and the blackjack tables. Businesses and agencies all over the west saved money scheduling annual meetings in Reno. Plus, their workers seemed to like it. Husbands all over the west liked it because it was the one time of the year where they could engage in safe sex with someone other than their wives, whom they had long since gotten bored with. Probably, many wives liked it too because they were freed up to fool around with whomever they wanted while hubby was away. The only losers were the poor schmucks who were nagged by their wives into bringing them along, so they could lounge by the pool or sit for hours at the slot machines while hubby was in meetings. Such men were rightfully shunned by their co-workers because their co-workers viewed these wives as spies, intruders who could destroy the only chance at sex that some of those men got each year.

The real Silver City was, of course, thirty miles south of Reno, a deserted ghost town, abandoned after the silver rush of the Comstock Lode discovery of 1859 fizzled out. If not for the steady stream of gamblers and husbands that the conventions brought in, Reno would face the same fate and end up a boarded-up forgotten footnote to silver fever.

It was the gambling business that had brought Dan Landes to Reno. Or rather, it was a job inside the gambling business that brought him there. Dan had been a detective in the Crenshaw District of Los Angeles, California, for years. He had specialized in white collar crime investigations, but had "retired" more than ten years ago, left the states, moved to Panama, and settled into the expatriate lifestyle. Initially, Panama seemed to suit him. He knew the lay of the land, having gone there for most of his vacations over many decades. He liked the laid-back culture, the friendly people, the weather, and the low cost of living. But last year things got rough, and he had returned to the U.S. to "get his bearings", as he told himself.

At first, he stayed with some old friends in Las Vegas. But Vegas was not the city he remembered. It had grown too big, too glitzy, into too much of a fantasy world—a city that had come to believe its own lies. He stayed with his friends long enough to get his armed security guard license from the state and to buy a used car. But when he got the offer to work security at Barkley's Casino Resort in Reno, he loaded up the car and drove there.

Compared to Vegas, Reno was actually a better fit for Dan, and Barkley's was almost a perfect fit. Because of his background, the casino hired him as part of their surveillance security, which suited Dan. He didn't want a high-pressure job, just something that provided a paycheck. He had only gotten the security guard license because law enforcement was the only thing he had ever done. He had no passion for it anymore, but it was the only thing he knew how to do, or was qualified to do. He was too old to go back to a police force, and besides, that was too dangerous. Casino surveillance security in Reno didn't pay well, but it was easy. There were only a set number of casino scams. Once you learned about them, they were easy to spot. Security cameras were everywhere, and Barkley's was not a big casino—there were only so many square feet of space inside the casino to patrol, and only so many hotel rooms to monitor. Plus, unlike most police departments, casino security was never understaffed—Nevada gambling regulations required a certain number of guards per square foot of casino space. Dan would spend four to five hours a day drinking coffee and watching video monitors of players at the tables or at the slot machines, and the rest of each day strolling around the casino floor. If he or one of the other surveillance security officers spotted someone cheating, the arrest was simple: they would notify the physical security guards and five of those guards would surround the cheater at the table or slot machine and, on a prearranged signal, they all would simply grab the cheater together, lift him out of his chair, and quickly carry him off to a detention room to wait for the police to arrive. The cheaters rarely put up a fight. Yes, casino security was easy, almost boring. It was the perfect occupation for Dan.

Truth be told, the part of the job that occupied most of his time, besides drinking coffee and staring at security monitors, was keeping track of the prostitutes. Prostitution was illegal in Reno, but legal in the neighboring city of Sparks, an anomaly that led all of the casinos to maintain a certain ecology—a certain balance—with the local hookers. As long as the hookers were discrete, they were tolerated. After all, the casinos figured, they were the reason many men still came to Reno. As long as the hookers didn't dress like hookers, as long as they fit in and gambled a little bit, and as long as they didn't steal from customers, the casinos let them be. The casinos didn't even mind if the gamblers took a break from the table and took a hooker up to their rooms, because the casinos had long since learned that once a man has had sex with a hooker at a casino, he will invariably return to the casino floor and gamble longer and more carelessly than ever. Something about sex loosens up a man's willingness to take chances.

So, part of Dan's job was spotting which women were prostitutes (which was easy since most of them were regulars) and then keeping an eye on them in case they picked up a john. There were cameras *everywhere* in the casino, except in the customers' rooms, so Dan could follow a particular hooker from the entrance to the casino, across the casino floor, to the tables, and from the tables past the lobby to the elevators, inside the elevators, and down the hotel hallways to the man's room. That's when the surveillance became important. Once they went inside the man's room, a camera was kept focused on that customer's hotel room door until the hooker left, and then until the man left and returned to the casino floor. If the hooker left, but the man didn't leave the room within the next fifteen minutes, the casino receptionist was instructed to call the man's room on a pretext—such as offering discounted tickets to a show—in order to determine that he was okay. If there was no answer, then security would get involved, sometimes with a follow-up "wrong number call" or sometimes with a mistaken room service delivery, until they determined that the man was safe. On the other hand, if the man left the casino with the hooker to go somewhere else, that was not the casino's problem.

All the professional hookers knew the set-up, and knew they could be identified, so robbery was seldom a problem. It was the meth-heads, first-time hookers, and strung-out lowlifes that would try something so stupid. But they were also easy to spot. They usually had the shakes or looked nervous, and they never gambled. With them, Dan's job was simply to go down to the casino floor, walk up to them, smile, and flash his badge. Usually, they got the message and left.

Yes, it was an easy job. But Reno was not where Dan wanted to end up. That was the problem. He didn't know where he wanted to end up, so Reno was as good of a place as any to sit and wait. When he first got to town, his funds were low, so he took a room at a run-down motel called Sheila's Inn. It was on the seedy side of town, which is to say it was just a few blocks from downtown. But it was cheap, and the room came with a hot plate and a small fridge. After Dan had made friends with the different clerks who worked the day and night shifts, he simply decided to stay there. Why sign a lease when he really didn't know how long he would stay in Reno? He worked out a decent monthly rate for the room—probably less than he would have had to pay for an apartment—because the motel liked having an armed security guard as a long-term tenant— so it worked out well. It was not where he wanted to end up, but it was okay for the moment. In some ways he felt lucky to find it. At least no one disturbed him there.

And Barkley's was not where he wanted to end

up either, but the problem was that he was good at the job. Maybe it was his background in analyzing financial records. Or maybe he was just lucky. But during his second week there, he stumbled upon a scam there that made him a favorite in the casino owners' eyes.

Barkley's, like all casinos, monitored its casino profits on a daily basis, not only for business purposes, but for security purposes. While individual cheaters will hit a casino one time and then disappear, an organized conspiracy, such as a skim, will hit the same casino every day for as long as the scam can last. And so it was with Barkley's. About a week before Dan was hired, the casino accountants started to notice a slight drop in profits. Individual gamblers rely on luck to turn a profit, but casinos rely on math, and long term casino earnings statistics are extremely consistent simply because the volume of business neutralizes any individual gambler's winning streak. Short term income trends, of course, are not as consistent, due to normal variations in casino daily profits depending on the day of the week, special promotions, holidays, etc. Thus, the owners weren't particularly concerned about this recent decline. But it seemed to be continuing, so they mentioned it to Abe Blair, the security manager, who brought it up at the daily meeting of all the security guards. That just happened to be Dan's second week on the job.

"So," Abe was saying, "the accountants were looking at yesterday's figures and noticed a slight drop in gaming income again. It's not much but it's the third week in a row that income has been down. They're somewhat baffled by this because our occupancy rate hasn't dropped, our buffet attendance is the same, our gaming tables seem to have the same number of players, and our slot usage is actually slightly up. The owners asked me if we had noticed anything different in the past couple of weeks and I told them we hadn't, but I said I would bring this to your attention."

There was a murmur in the group. A couple of the

guards said that they hadn't noticed anything unusual. Then Dan raised his hand.

"How much is the loss?" he asked.

"Well, it varies day by day," Abe said, looking at his handwritten notes. "Some days it's around two percent, other days it's up to four percent."

"That's a percentage of that day's gaming income, right?" Dan asked.

"Uh huh," Abe responded.

"What does that percentage translate to in actual daily dollar amounts?" Dan asked.

"Ah, they didn't give me that information."

"Ok, well, do they know what area the loss is coming from? I mean, is it from the craps games or blackjack, or the slots?" Dan asked.

"I understand they are working on analyzing that," Abe said.

"Hmm. Okay, thanks. Just curious," Dan said.

The rest of the meeting turned to other topics. That morning, Dan did his usual routine of drinking coffee and watching the monitors. He spotted one fellow at the roulette game "topping the chips", meaning, placing a $500 chip on a column bet but covering it with a sloppy stack of $1 chips to hide the $500 chip. If the ball landed any one of the twelve numbers in the cheater's chosen column, his bet would pay two-to-one. The croupier would discover the $500 chip when he picked up the cheater's bet and would be required to pay; but if the ball landed on a number in a different column, the cheater would quickly remove the $500 chip from the bottom of the stack while an accomplice at the table created a distraction by spilling a drink or yelling or throwing some chips. Although it's a well-known con, it's difficult to prove because security has to catch the cheater actually removing the higher-value chip. If the cheater wins, he collects his money and he's usually out the door quickly. If he loses his bet, he's only out a couple of dollars, but he also usually leaves (to go to a different casino), because to try the same distraction a second time at the same roulette wheel would raise suspicion. The trick to catching a "topper", Dan figured, was to focus on every new player's first few bets. If they came to the table early, but bet late, acting like they were being distracted, and especially if they placed a pile of chips in a sloppy fashion on a column bet, an odd/even bet, or a red/black bet, then Dan would grab the camera controls and zoom one camera in on the chips and one camera on the bettor. If his bet won, and it turned out there was a high value chip at the bottom of the bet, there was nothing Dan could do but log the incident and add the photo of the cheater's face to the log of suspected cheaters that was shared with all the other casinos in Nevada. But if the cheater lost and the cameras could catch him in the act of removing the chip, then he could be arrested, maybe prosecuted, but definitively barred from all the casinos in town. On that particular day, Dan was lucky. The angle of the camera zooming in on the stack of chips clearly caught the color of the $500 chip—out of sight from the croupier, but in sight of the camera's zoom lens. The man's bet lost. Someone at the table pretended to trip and fall, and the other camera captured the cheater's hand quickly swiping the $500 chip off the table before the croupier could collect the losing bets. As Dan was talking to the physical security guards on the walkie-talkie, telling them which man to arrest, he was thinking to himself that he had to hand it to the man's skill at sleight-of-hand. If it wasn't for the camera catching, he wouldn't have seen it. He even had to rewind the digital recording and play it back in slow motion to confirm the cheat. But there it was, quick and precise.

Later that afternoon, Abe Blair dropped by to congratulate Dan. "I talked to the D.A.," Abe was saying. "You know, it's usually difficult to prosecute a guy for trying to steal a single chip, but it turns out that this guy has convictions in two other states for doing the same thing. So the D.A. says he can charge him with felony fraud."

"Interesting," Dan said. "It's a shame, really. The guy's hand control was so good, so quick, that he would have made a great slight-of-hand magician."

"Yeah, but he probably made more money this way," Abe said.

Dan nodded his head.

"But on another note, Dan, I talked to the accountants about what you asked this morning, and they went back and looked at the figures. They had only been looking at percentages, but when they looked at actual dollar amounts, they found that the daily shortfall from the usual gaming income has been averaging $2800 every day. On a slow day, the gaming floor takes in $70,000. But that can double on a weekend–that's why the percentage of loss varied. But for the past three weeks, no matter what the total daily intake had been, we've been down approximately $2800 a day from this same time period last year, even when adjusted for the yearly differences. Plus, they finished their analysis of the area of loss, and it's all coming from the slot machines. Your questions were right on. They're now convinced there's some type of fraud happening in the slot area, but they don't know what it is. We've had the I.T. guys check every slot machine this morning, and they all seem to be working correctly. None of them are showing any abnormally large payouts. I'm going to discuss it at tomorrow morning's meeting. I just thought I'd let you know in advance."

"Ok, thanks Abe," Dan said. "I'll keep an eye out this afternoon."

But Dan saw nothing unusual on the surveillance monitors that afternoon. The slot machine traffic seemed normal. Slots are the single most lucrative part of any casino—they comprise ninety percent of a casino's profits. The ads for casinos might show smiling faces at the craps table, but it's the slot machines that bring the gamers in; which is why Barkley's, like every other casino, had more floor space devoted to slot machines than any other game. There was even a slot machine in the bathrooms on the casino floor. The sheer number of machines always presented a challenge for surveillance, which is why most slot surveillance consisted of looking for unusual movements at the machine. Playing a slot machine is relative simple: The player sits down and inserts money, usually dollar bills or occasionally a payout slip from another machine, and then hits the Spin button repeatedly, much like what a monkey would do. The only deviations from these movements are to take a sip from their drink, or to light a cigarette, or to insert more money. When they're done playing, they either shake their heads and leave, or the lucky few take a payout slip and go to the cashier window. With so many players to keep an eye on, what most security guards do is look for anomalies—someone fiddling with the machine, or sitting in such a way as to obscure what they are doing. Older machines had a drop slot where coins would fall if a player won. But these were susceptible to the use of "wands", basically laser lights that a cheater could insert up the drop slot to confuse the electric eye in the machine so it wouldn't know how many coins it had already dropped and would continue dropping coins. So Barkley's, like most casinos, had switched to machines that displayed the player's winnings on the screen but paid out on a paper slip only when the player hit the payout button.

That afternoon, Dan watched the slot players from all the different surveillance cameras. But he saw no suspicious activity. It was getting late in the day, and he was tired. So, for the last hour, he just stared at one camera and kept his eyes unfocused, just looking at the pattern of the players. They seemed to move like fallen leaves on sidewalks, as if invisible puffs of wind were blowing them around. Some would be blown off their chairs and tumble through the casino, and then a new group of leaves would be blown into their vacant seats. And their clothes reminded Dan of dead leaves, too. For some reason, Dan had noticed, gamblers always seem to wear dark clothes. In his unfocused gaze, there was just a constant rhythmic movement of crumbled brown leaves being blown in puffs around the casino floor.

When his shift ended, Dan clocked out, stopped by the liquor store for a bottle, and then walked back to Sheila's Inn. One thing he liked about that old motel was that he could walk to work. Sheila's was one of those old-style "motor inns" where the rooms were arranged in a horseshoe shape around the parking lot, so Dan could leave his car parked right in front of his room. He liked that he was saving on gas money, and the motel staff also liked that he left his car there during the day. It gave the impression that the place might be popular.

Chapter 2

Once Dan got inside his motel room, he started to fill the bathtub with hot water. He liked soaking in a hot bath the first thing after work. Well... he liked drinking while he soaked in a hot bath the first thing after work. The combination of alcohol and hot water seemed to wash away the mental grime and dust that always accumulated from working an eight hour shift.

It wasn't Dan's original plan to go back to working a real job at his age. He had had a pretty good deal down in Panama. He had settled a wrongful discharge/retaliation claim against the L.A. police department years ago, and for political reasons they agreed to structure the settlement as an early retirement pension, so that he was able to afford to move to Panama. That money was deposited monthly in his Panamanian bank account. Because of the lower cost of living in Panama, that money was enough to pay all his basic expenses and more. Once he moved down there, and settled in the small town of Villa Rosario, he found a part-time job working for a sportsbook company named Berghoff's. Ironically, because of his police training in computers and financial analysis, he was able to make good money in the online betting industry which was legal in Panama but illegal in the U.S. His monthly commissions for working two hours a day on the sportsbook website from his apartment in Panama almost equaled his police pension. So the combination of both incomes allowed him to live extremely well. Dan himself never gambled, but he was good at analyzing the ebbs and flows of gambling data. That was another reason Barkley's Casino had hired him.

The tub was full. Dan tested the water with his hand. Nice and hot. He got undressed, poured himself a drink in a tall glass, and carefully stepped into the tub and eased himself down.

He didn't like to think how it all had come crashing down last year. He knew he needed to think about it—the reason he left Panama and came back to the states was to process it—but it all still felt too raw. It hadn't bothered him that Berghoff's had gone under. He always knew that day was coming. Even though online betting was legal in Panama, the owners and all the bet collectors were in the U.S., so it was just a matter of time before the U.S. feds indicted them. That effectively shut down Berghoff's. But, as said, Dan had foreseen that. He personally hadn't broken any laws and besides, he made sure that there was nothing to connect him to Berghoff's. He always connected to their computer through a proxy server in Venezuela; he never dealt with the actual bets the U.S. gamblers were making; he only analyzed the data for the local managers; there was no paper or digital trail to connect him to the business; and Berghoff's always paid him in cash. He hadn't been a cop for twenty years for nothing. No, it didn't bother him that Berghoff's had crashed and burned. It was the other thing that haunted him.

He took a sip of his drink and held the liquor in his mouth. It was funny, he thought, how certain habits are so attached to certain locations. In Panama, he usually only drank beer. But as soon as he got to the states, he switched back to sour mash whiskey, a drink he hadn't touched in more than a decade. He could have gotten it easily in Panama, but he never wanted it there. But once he hit the states, it was the only thing he wanted to drink, because that's what he used to drink when he lived in the states. He wondered if remorse was the same way. Did it hover over certain places like smoke… like clouds hovering over the Smoky Mountains? When he got back to the states, the pain he had felt in Panama seemed to go away. But he knew it would be waiting for him in Panama as soon as he returned, as soon as he stepped off the plane. He wondered again how long he would stay in the states. "Well," he thought to himself, "long enough until I can figure this out. Then I'm going back." He swallowed, and let that potent sweet burning fluid slide down his throat, warming his chest all the way down.

When he left Panama, he had decided to let his monthly pension payments just accrue in his Panamanian bank account while he was gone, on the theory that he needed to work a job in the U.S. to structure his time. Too much unstructured time is not good when you're going through shit, he had told himself. A person needs to be forced to think about other things, practical things, like putting food on the table. So he had brought only enough money with him to support himself in Vegas while he got current on licenses and looked for a job. That process took longer than he had anticipated. In fact, the Barkley's gig had come along just in time.

He turned the hot water tap back on and raised the temperature in the tub just a bit. Yes, the Barkley's job had come along just in the nick of time. That was lucky, he thought. Sometimes we forget how lucky we are. He took another sip of whiskey and held the fluid in his mouth again, leaned his head carefully against the edge of the tub, lowering his body down a bit, and closed his eyes. He could feel the worries of the day seeping out of his pores. The thought crossed his mind again that the gamblers he had seen on the screen that afternoon were all dressed in dark colors. Why was that? Were they trying to be incognito? Well, he could understand that. No one wants to stand out. He never wanted to stand out—he just wanted to be a good cop back in L.A. But they fucked that up for him; he just wanted to be a good expat down in Panama but don Fernando had fucked that up for him... well, no, that wasn't true. Don Fernando hadn't fucked that up. It was Dan himself, and his stupid naiveté that had fucked it up. He had been torpedoed by his own naiveté But he didn't want to think about it now. So he thought again about all the gamblers floating around the casino floor in brown clothes, dark slacks, dark t-shirts, dark polo shirts, dark dresses, all looking darkly glum, darkly determined, darkly depressed. The only colors in the scene were the short red frilly skirts of the cocktail waitresses or the white payout slips that a few players clutched in their determined little hands... Dan took another sip of whiskey. Even with his eyes closed, he knew exactly where his mouth was. "Ah, sweet whiskey," he mused to himself, "that doth knit up the raveled sleeve of care..." Who had said that? Oh yeah, Shakespeare... but of course he wasn't talking about whiskey. Dan let the sip of whiskey slide down his throat. He felt warm and magical inside. Soon the image of the dark-clothed gamblers drained from his mind and seeped away. The whiskey or the hot water, or both, were working their magic once again. He took a deep breath and felt himself relaxing. Random images floated through his mind: women he had known, other places he had drank whiskey, fragments of songs, an image of a field where he used to play as a child... But Dan didn't want to fall asleep in the tub. Besides, the water was starting to lose its warmth. He opened his eyes, looked around, and began to pull himself out of the tub. He was starting to feel hungry, and began to wonder if he had any food left in the refrigerator. He had forgotten to stop and get any groceries on the walk home.

He dried himself and checked the refrigerator. Fuck. He thought he had some ham and bread left, but he remembered he had used those to make a sandwich to take to work that day. He made a mental note to buy some groceries tomorrow. But now, he needed to weigh his options for tonight. There was a diner down the block—a greasy steak and eggs kind of place. Or he could use his employee discount at the casino buffet, and for the same amount of money get a healthy meal. He really hated the idea of going back to the casino. He would have preferred to cook in the motel room, but given the choices, it made the most economic sense to go back to the casino. Damn his rational brain—always analyzing the data. He really didn't want to go back there tonight. But he put on a pair of jeans and a t-shirt—what he called his off-duty uniform—and got ready to leave.

As Dan opened the motel room door, he noticed that a vehicle had parked next to his. It was an old red VW bus. He didn't think they made those anymore. It looked like the second door on the passenger side was open. Dan was just standing there looking at it when he realized that there was a young woman bending over in front of that open door. She was lifting a cardboard box, and was starting to carry it around the front of the bus. It was then that Dan saw that the door to the motel room next to his was also open. This woman was moving into that room.

"Need any help?" Dan asked, almost automatically.

"No, thanks, I got it," the girl said and walked into her room.

Okay, thought Dan, as he turned around to lock his door. He was turning back around, ready to leave, when the girl stepped out of her room and said, "Hi, my name's Sara," and held out her hand. It almost startled Dan. But he shook her hand and replied, "Mine's Dan, glad to meet you."

"How long are you in town for?" she asked.

"Well," Dan replied, fumbling for words, "actually kind of indefinitely, I'm sort of living here for the moment."

"Really? This place that good?" Sara asked with a smile.

"Well, it's quiet," Dan said.

"Well, nice to meet you," Sara said, "I got to get back to unloading."

"Ok, well good luck... nice to meet you too," Dan said as he walked away. He considered asking again if she needed any help, but decided against it, and began the four block walk to the casino.

"Pretty girl," he thought to himself, "nice wholesome smile... wonder what the fuck's she doing in Reno." He put her age at about thirty but wasn't sure why—she actually looked younger—but he generally trusted his first impression of someone's age.

He knew that stepping inside of the casino door, and being engulfed by the clanging soundtrack of the slot machine bells, the yelling from the craps table, the unidentifiable musical sounds, and the stale recycled air-conditioned air would instantly undo all the relaxation he had spent the last forty-five minutes achieving. But now he was very hungry, so he steeled himself, half-closed his eyes, and walked through the revolving door. The wave of sound, sights, and smells did indeed cascade over him as he knew it would, but he made his way across the casino floor towards the stairs in the center of the casino that led to the buffet on the second floor. At least in the buffet dining area, the sound was more muted, and the air seemed cleaner. He didn't need to show his employee ID to the cashier—she knew him. He paid the discounted fee and the hostess showed him to a table. As he had predicted, at least he could eat well here, and he did. But he wished he could have gotten a to-go box and taken it all back to his motel room, but he knew they didn't allow that. So Dan ate his fill, left a tip, and headed out.

As he walked down the stairs to the casino floor, he was looking forward to just stretching out on his bed, pouring himself another glass of whiskey and just relaxing in private. He hoped that Sara wasn't going to be a noisy neighbor. But as he got to the casino floor and began to walk through the slots area, he slowed his pace and looked around. Maybe it was the benefit of a full stomach, or maybe it was his detective brain, but he stopped and looked at the people. They really were all wearing dark clothes. He turned around and looked at the crowd by the craps table and at the blackjack tables—they all seemed to be wearing dark clothes, too. "That's so odd," he thought to himself. "Why have I never noticed that before?"

He turned towards the slot machines again. "What a monotonous game," he thought to himself.

Yet he knew that for many people it was an addiction stronger than heroin. He watched the sea of people resting their right forearms on the machine, first two fingers raised, hitting that Spin button over and over. Every other second, one of the machines would ring bells, signaling that the bet had paid off some amount—it might be paying off less than the amount that was bet, but it would ring that bell anyway. That was the beautiful illusion that the slot machines gave—making the players think they were winning even when they were actually losing.

He watched one older woman near him hit the payout button on her machine. A long white slip of paper spit out, with her total "winnings" in big numbers and a bar code at the bottom of the slip that the cashier would scan to verify the amount. The lady turned to the other older woman sitting next to her and yelled, "I'm going to try my luck on the Wheel of Fortune." The other woman nodded without looking up, and the first woman walked over to an empty Wheel of Fortune slot machine and fed the paper ticket in and started betting.

One of the barbacks—a woman named Ashley, whom Dan knew—was walking through the casino. She was probably getting off her shift, Dan assumed. She spotted him, smiled and started to wave, but then furrowed her brow and walked quietly up to him.

"Are you working undercover?" she whispered while pretending not to look at him.

Dan laughed, "No. I just forgot to buy groceries for dinner so I came over to eat upstairs."

She looked relieved, and said, "I have just never seen you in jeans before. I thought maybe I was supposed to ignore you."

Dan smiled at her. "No, I don't do any undercover stuff. At least they haven't asked me to. I assume it's because I look too much like a cop."

Now it was Ashley's turn to laugh. "Yeah, well, yeah, you kinda do. Are you heading out?"

"No, I'm going to watch this area just a bit more."

Ashley furrowed her brow again. "Then you are working?"

"No, I'm just trying to figure something out."

"Yeah, that's called working. Be careful, or you'll burn out. Once my shift is over, I'm outta here."

"You're probably right, but I'm just going to watch a bit more. You have a good night, Ashley."

"You too, Dan."

Dan watched her walk away, and thought to himself, "That's the second pretty woman I've talked to tonight. Why are they always so damn young?"

He turned his gaze back to the slots. The older lady at the Wheel of Fortune machine stood up and said "damn" in a loud voice and slammed her palm against the payout button. Another white slip appeared. She grabbed it and walked back over to the original machine she had been playing, next to her friend. The seat was still vacant. As she sat down she shouted to her friend, "That machine was worse than this one!" Her friend continued hitting the Spin button, but nodded her head without looking up. The first woman fed her new payout slip into the slot machine. The balance showed on her screen, and she started playing.

Dan's brain was now totally sober and absorbed by the flow of paper. He had spent the afternoon watching people move from machine to machine. But now, in his mind's eye, he was seeing the flow of payout slips from machine to machine. There had to be triple, maybe quadruple the number of payout slips in the bins inside the slot machines versus what the cashiers received. A player might play six or seven machines in an evening, generating a payout slip from each machine which was inserted into to another slot machine to start playing again, long before the player ever finished for the evening and took his final payout slip (assuming he had one) to the cashier.

Dan knew the cashiers kept the payout tickets that the players used to cash out their winnings. He wasn't sure how long they were kept or where they were stored. But he knew that the accountants would compare them with the slot machines that issued them, to make sure they were accurate. The barcodes at the bottom of each ticket contained a lot of information besides the amount of the payout. They also contained the identity of which machine issued them, a time/date stamp, and the customer's "Players Club" card number, assuming the player had used a Players Club card. Most of the regular slot players used them, and would insert them every time they played, because extended slot machine play generated comps for the players, like free meals, free spins, and entry into drawings for prizes.

But Dan didn't know how often the accountants audited the payout slips. He only knew that it was a quick process, so he assumed it was a frequent, if not a daily process. Slot machines are basically computers. Each one is connected to a server in the accounting office. The accountants needed only to feed the payout slips into the scanner slot of the server, and the server would instantly compare that slip with the data record of the slot machine that issued it. The authenticity of the payout slips could be checked as fast as those payout slips could be fed into the scanner slot.

But Dan was wondering what happened to the payout slips that players themselves fed into the slot machines? If there was something defective about that payout slip, the slot machine would simply reject it and spit it back out to the player. But if the machine accepted it, the player could play with the amount of credit on that ticket, and the used payout slip would fall into a bin inside the slot machine. Dan didn't know what happened to those used payout slips. No one had ever mentioned them. He made a mental note to ask Abe at tomorrow's meeting.

Dan shook his head to stop his brain from thinking. Ashley was right—this *was* working. He turned and walked out of the casino and headed back towards the motel. He decided to stop by a quick market on the way and get some groceries.

He could learn from Ashley, he thought.
Clock out, get out, and stay out.

Chapter 3

That night Dan had that dream again. At first it was just a normal dream. He was standing on the casino floor, just watching all the gamblers swirling around him. But then things began to speed up, or rather, all the players seemed to speed up. It was as if he was stuck in time but the gamblers were in fast motion, and getting faster. They bounced from machine to machine, from table to table, like pinballs, ricocheting off each machine, moving faster and faster, becoming a blur until finally the blackjack tables exploded and a shower of cards cascaded over him. And then he was back in Panama. He was in that police station in La Chorrera, standing next to don Fernando, the police chief of the nearby village of Villa Rosario. They were standing in front of several jail cells. The cells were empty except for one prisoner who was standing there, grinning at them through the bars. Don Fernando was pulling his revolver out of his holster. The next thing Dan knew, the prisoner's chest exploded in red and he crumpled backwards, his hands flailing at the air. Then suddenly Dan was stuck in time again. But everything seemed to be going in slow motion. Another bullet slowly peeled off the side of the prisoner's head. Dan could see the eggshell thin skull fracture and slowly explode outward. Blood and gray matter and paper-white shards of skull floated back through the air and splattered against the concrete wall of the cell.

It was the same dream… always the same dream. It always started with something else, then abruptly shifted to La Chorrera. Dan woke up angry. It had been his own damn fault— his own foolish mistake to assume that morality was somehow universal. It wasn't. Either it was different everywhere or else there was no morality anywhere. His head hurt. He looked at the clock. 5:30

a.m. He got up and stepped into the bathroom and splashed some water on his face. He opened the cabinet and got the ibuprofen bottle and poured two pills out of the bottle. Then he went to the compact refrigerator in the other room and took out the loaf of bread he had bought on his way home last night and ate a slice to buffer his stomach and then he took the ibuprofen with some water. Moving around seemed to ground him, and made him feel better. The image of that jail cell in La Chorrera began to fade a bit.

It had been almost five months since don Fernando had asked his help in solving a murder back in La Chorrera. Homicides were not Dan's area of expertise. But don Fernando was a friend, so Dan agreed to help. He had been friends with don Fernando for almost ten years. They had been good friends, and so Dan thought he understood don Fernando, thought he understood his thinking and his culture. What an amateur mistake that had been, he now realized. You can never really understand someone from another culture because it's impossible to really know another culture. You can know *facts* about another culture. You can speak the language—Dan spoke Spanish well—but the deep-down subtle undercurrents of any culture are beyond comprehension. Dan had helped don Fernando, and the suspect was soon caught, partly because of Dan's help and partly, like most police work, because of some lucky breaks. Dan had assumed his job was done, as it would have been done in the states, and that the Panamanian courts would take care of the trial and resolution of the case. Dan had no doubt that the suspect was guilty, but because of—or maybe in spite of—all his years as a detective in the Crenshaw District, he still had faith in justice, and in the judicial system. But Dan didn't know that honor killing was allowed in Panama. The family of the victim that the suspect had murdered made the ancient traditional request to don Fernando, and so don Fernando had arranged for the suspect to be murdered in his jail cell. Everyone knew what had happened, but it didn't upset anyone. It was just the way things were done there. The other policemen in the station all knew. The victim's family knew. The newspapers probably knew, but simply reported that the suspect was shot trying to escape. Unfortunately Dan was there to see what actually had happened. Otherwise, he was sure don Fernando would have looked him straight in the face and told him that the man tried to escape. Dan had witnessed a cold blooded murder and everyone around him acted like it was nothing out of the ordinary. And what ate at Dan was that it was his own detective work that had helped make that murder possible.

He looked the clock again. 5:45 a.m. His headache was starting to dissipate. He might as well make breakfast, he thought. He placed a coffee filter in the cheap Mr. Coffee and filled it with ground coffee, filled the machine with water, and turned it on. Maybe coffee would help.

Dan had known police officers in the Crenshaw District of Los Angeles who had broken the law. Hell, he had certainly pushed the law right up to that invisible line a few times himself, but he always felt that he had had a private moral code that had kept him honest. But ever since La Chorrera, he wasn't so sure anymore.

He got two strips of bacon from the package in the refrigerator, laid them in the frying pan and turned the hot plate on. At first he had tried to rationalize what don Fernando had done. Dan remembered a cop named William Grizzard back in Crenshaw. Will was a nice guy, a laid back kind of guy, easy to hang out with, and Dan had drank many beers with him even though the word around the station was that Will would occasionally plant drugs on suspects he arrested just to make the arrest stronger. But Dan didn't work directly with Will; never saw Will do that; never asked him about it; and so it was easy to hang out with him. That was the thing about police culture—you overlooked the occasional illegality because you were all fighting a common enemy. If it was for the greater good of getting bad guys off the street, and if you didn't personally see it, you just let it pass and didn't talk about it. But now, Dan had to ask himself: how was what Will did any different from what don Fernando had done? Well, the difference was that Dan had witnessed it firsthand.

Dan cracked two eggs open and stirred them into the bacon. The hotplate only had one burner, so Dan cooked everything in one frying pan. He reached into the compact refrigerator, took out a packet of shredded cheese, tore open the package and sprinkled cheese over the top of the bubbling egg/bacon mixture.

Will eventually got busted when a rookie partner ratted him out for planting a gun on a suspect. Will took a demotion and was transferred to a different district. At the time, no one criticized Will. But everyone shunned the rookie cop and refused to partner with him, until the rookie quit. Ironically, that was only a few months before Dan had gotten accused of tipping off a gang of drug dealers about an upcoming raid. The accusation was totally false, but the same shunning and retaliation happened to him that had happened to the rookie. He was amazed how quickly his friends had turned on him. It really opened his eyes and made him start questioning the police culture he had believed in. After the evidence showed he was innocent, he got a good lawyer and negotiated his "retirement pension" in lieu of suing the police department. They didn't want the publicity, and Dan just wanted enough money so he could move to Panama and not do any more police work.

Dan stirred the eggs one more time, turned the burner off, and slid the scrambled egg/bacon/cheese mixture onto a piece of bread on a plate. He wanted to buy a toaster but he knew they made too many crumbs and would attract mice. That's why he had to keep the bread in the refrigerator. Mice... well, whaddya want for cheap rent, he had told himself. He poured himself a cup of coffee and sat down on the bed to eat his breakfast.

Maybe it's the nature of man to always do evil, he thought. Maybe the ancient theologians were right—

that life was a constant battle between good and evil, with evil always holding the upper hand. Maybe, he thought, life was just one big casino, where the odds were always stacked against you. Maybe you thought it was your skill in avoiding evil, but it was just your luck, just like the blackjack players who always bragged of how skillfully they played their hands when they won big, but always blamed bad luck when they lost.

Dan really liked Panama—he thought he would never leave. But something about seeing the murder of that suspect in La Chorrera—just 10 feet away from where he was standing—had just totally fucked with Dan's head. Maybe it was seeing someone get shot; maybe he just wasn't hardened enough; after all, his police work had always been in the office, analyzing spreadsheets and hard drives, looking for money laundering , looking for fraud. He had seen murder victims, accident victims, but all after the fact. He had never witnessed someone being killed in cold blood. But regardless, he just couldn't stay in Panama after that. So he came back to the states—to think and clear his head. He wanted to go back to Panama—he certainly didn't fit in the U.S. anymore—and he knew he would go back at some point; he just wasn't sure when. He explained to his landlord in Panama that he was going to take a long vacation, and he prepaid the rest of the year's rent. Rent was cheap in Panama and the landlord was glad to have such an advance, and promised Dan he would keep the apartment and all of Dan's belongings secure while he was gone.

Dan finished his breakfast, washed the plate and the frying pan in the bathroom sink and placed them on the counter by the hotplate to dry. He poured himself another cup of coffee and then stretched out on the bed. The way the rooms were laid out in this motel, the bathroom in Sara's room next door butted up against the wall next to his headboard. He heard her open her bathroom door and then heard her pee in the toilet. He knew that she didn't know how thin the walls were. She would probably be appalled. He imagined her sitting there on the toilet and wondered what, if anything, she was wearing. She sure was cute. He heard the toilet flush, but then nothing else. He guessed she was going back to bed. He took another sip of coffee and looked at the clock. Shit. He still had two more hours before he had to clock in. Well, hell, that's better than being rushed. He rested the coffee cup on his chest and thought about the day before. It hadn't been a bad day, really. He had caught a topper, had been complimented by Abe, had met Sara and chatted with Ashley, plus he had had a nice dinner at the casino buffet. That wasn't a bad day at all. He certainly had suffered through much worse days since he had returned to the states. Plus, Abe had given him something challenging to think about: if there was a fraud, how could someone be ripping off the slot machines every day? And why the same amount every day? Why $2800? Dan knew one of the cardinal rules of successful fraud was "small amounts"—always do the skim in small enough amounts so that no one's suspicions are ever aroused. So what was it about $2800 that fit that rule? 2800, 2800... math computations started to appear in his mind. 2800 divided in half is 1400... 1400 divided in half is 700... 700 divided in half is 350... 350 divided in half is 175...

He sat up in bed, almost spilling his coffee. $175! Just five dollars below the limit where the cashier would have been required by the casino's rules to get a manager to sign off on the payout slip! How many times would a person have to take a $175 slip to a cashier in a day to collect $2800? It would take 16 trips. That would stand out. So it had to be a team, but how many? Two people could make eight trips to the cashier with a $175 payout slip—still too obvious. Four people would have to make four trips... but eight people could only have to make 2 trips a day. And there were three different sets of cashier windows in the casino. A person could hit different cashiers at different windows at different times in the day, and as long as the payout slip was authentic and under $180, the cashier would simply pay them and they'd be gone…. As long as the payout slip was authentic… and the payout slips had to be authentic because the accountants checked them, right? Again, he made a mental note to ask Abe about that. His brain kept processing. You'd have to keep changing the team because one, two, even four people—over time— would stand out to the cashiers. Yes, there are regular slot players—the buses from the nearby nursing homes and retirement communities pulled up every day and dumped the old people out, many in wheelchairs and walkers, but still they never missed a day—but you don't have regular winners. Some granny with a cane might hit a $200 jackpot once a month, after she had spent $500 that month, but that was as frequent as any one person might win. Nobody won every day.

Dan wondered if a team of eight people would stand out. Would some cashier notice the same people winning every day if those people were going to different cashiers each time? Or what if the team was bigger? Sixteen people would only have to cash out a winning $175 payout slip once a day… but that's a lot of people. And they wouldn't fit in that easily, Dan thought. Dan's experience was that the average age of a person who commits a fraud was around thirty. Sixteen 30-year-olds might stand out among the white-haired seniors that made up the majority of slot players. And what would such a large group do during the rest of the day? Maybe they were hitting all the casinos in town. That's another thing to ask Abe, Dan thought to himself.

His brain was firing on all cylinders now, just like the old days. "Shit," he thought to himself, "this is pointless—I might as well go into work early and write all this stuff down and send Abe an email."

He took a final sip of coffee and got up from the bed and headed into the bathroom to shower and shave.

Chapter 4

"I read your email," Abe was saying to Dan later that morning."I asked the accountants about the payout slips. It turns out that they've only been checking the payout slips over $180. They used to run them all through the server, but we remodeled the west side about three months ago, took out a bunch of baccarat and pai gow tables, and added about forty slot machines, which increased the number of payout slips. The accountants couldn't justify the extra time checking them all, since there never seemed to be a problem with them, so they changed the protocol to check only the higher payout slips."

"I see," said Dan. "And what about the payout slips inside the slot machines?"

"Well, they've never checked those except to audit a machine that seems to be malfunctioning—there's just too many of those slips to check."

"I see," said Dan again, nodding his head,

"But I could ask them to do a special audit for a few days, and check all of the payout slips from the cashiers," Abe said.

Dan's head was still nodding as if to signal yes, but his brain was thinking.

"No... no," Dan said, "don't do that..."

"But I thought you thought..." Abe started to say.

"No," Dan interrupted. "What I mean is, don't ask them to audit the slips from the cashier windows. Ask them to just audit all the slips from inside the machines."

"What?"

"Well, I've been thinking, Abe. Maybe I'm totally off the mark... but if there is a group that is systematically cheating the casino using payout slips, they're not doing it with the payout slips that they give to the cashiers."

"I don't understand," Abe said.

"Well, what does the data on the payout slip actually contain? It only tells the server which machine that ticket came from, and what the payout amount was."

"Plus the Players Club number," added Abe.

"But the cheaters wouldn't use a Players Club number," Dan responded, "because it would identify them. So the only useful information on the slip will be which machine created the ticket. If a cashier gives a payout slip to one of the accountants to run through the server, what does the server do? It communicates with that machine on the floor to verify if that machine actually created that ticket. That's all the slip would tell us. Well, if I'm a scam artist sophisticated enough to create a fraud using payout slips, then I'm going to know that I could be caught by giving the cashier a payout slip that would show that it wasn't created by a slot machine on the floor. I would want to give the cashier a legitimate payout slip."

"You think someone's counterfeiting the payout slips they give to the cashiers?"

"No, no, just the opposite," Dan said. "But yes, I am wondering if there are counterfeit slips. But if there are, they're not at the cashier windows—they're in the machines. Look, I've been watching the slots monitors all morning, or rather... watching the people who come into the casino to play the slot machines all morning. The only people who walk into the casino and walk straight up to the cashier windows are those people who are buying chips. Nobody comes into the casino and walks straight up to cashier window to present a payout slip."

"Well, right," Abe said, "of course."

"No, but I *would* do that if I was going to hand a counterfeit payout slip to a cashier. I would walk in, get my money, and walk out as quickly as possible. But no one does that. The people who walk into the casino intending to play slots walk straight over to the slots and wander around until they pick out, you know, their *lucky machine.*" Dan made air quotes with his fingers on the last two words, then continued. "But suppose I do have a counterfeit payout slip. What can I do with it? Well, if I know they never check the payout slips *inside* the machines, I can feed it into the machine, get all my credits, play for a minute or two, then print out a new payout slip, and take that payout slip to the cashier. If they were to check *that* payout slip, it would be legitimate, because the slot machine would tell the server, 'yes, I printed that ticket for that amount.'"

"I see," Abe said.

"Was there another $2800 loss yesterday?" Dan asked.

"Yup."

"Have them process all the payout slips that were inside the machine from yesterday."

"Ok, I will." Abe said.

Dan pointed to one of the monitors. "I got thinking about this because I watched two people this morning walk into the casino, at different times, each walk over to one of the machines away from the foot traffic and other people. Both pulled a payout slip from their pockets, fed it into the machine, did one spin, then hit the payout button, got a new slip, took it to the cashier, got their money and left the casino. Here, let me show you." Dan hit some buttons and the computer that stored the digital images of that morning's camera recordings rewound to a point that Dan had marked earlier that morning.

"See this guy, walking in? He goes straight over to this bank of slots, sits here, away from the aisle machines. He's dressed in dark clothes, just like all the other players... nothing unusual. But watch... he looks around, pulls out a white payout slip from his pocket, kinda hides it, and feeds it into the machine... See? Then he hits the Spin button one time, but doesn't win anything. Now watch... he hits the payout button, gets a new payout slip, and gets up. Now he walks over to the cashier... here, that's on a different camera..." Dan pushed some more buttons and a different camera angle appeared on the screen showing the man walking up to a cashier. "See? He cashes out his ticket and then turns and walks out of the casino." Dan hit some more buttons and a different camera showed the man walking out thought the revolving door. Dan adjusted the dials again. "Now watch... a few minutes later, this woman walks in, kinda shabbily dressed, but again, nothing really unusual. She walks straight to the machines, and also selects one in a row where no one else is sitting. Now she inserts some money. See? Let me rewind and zoom in. You can see here she's inserting a five-dollar bill in the quarter machine... now watch. She plays until that money is gone. I almost dismissed her as a regular player this morning, but watch—she then pulls a payout slip from her purse and inserts that into the machine. See? She hits one spin, just like that first guy, loses that bet, and then hits the payout button and gets a new slip. Now she stands up, and walks straight to the cashier window, a cashier window on a different side of the casino from where she was playing, not the nearest cashier, you see..." Dan pushed some more buttons. "And here you see her getting her money, and then she leaves."

Abe watched the video of the woman leaving the casino. "Well, I'll be damned," he said under his breath.

"It was those two people who got me thinking that if there are counterfeit slips, they're inside the machines. Actually it was the woman who got me thinking. I couldn't understand why someone would play with cash when they had a valuable payout slip in their pocket. The only reason they would do that would be to give the appearance of having been playing for awhile. If she had been lucky, her five dollar bill might have stretched into 10 minutes of play and I would have stopped watching her.

Abe straightened up and said, "I'm going to go talk to the accountants right now."

"Oh," Dan said. "Did you ask them about other casinos?"

"I mentioned that to them, but now I'm going to make sure they check with every casino in town, and have them audit their daily intake from the slots area and look for a daily loss of $2800."

"Well, hang on..." Dan said. "Let me think... I would just ask them to check for a consistent daily dollar amount loss. It may not be $2800. It's possible that some of the casinos have different policies about checking payout slips. Maybe some casinos check payout slips over $150 or over $100... If this whole crazy hypothesis is true, then their daily loss would be five dollars below whatever amount their policy says they have to check, times sixteen... I figure whoever's in charge is going to use the same team of sixteen people at all the casinos. So if their policy is to check every payout slip over $150, then the loss should be $145 times sixteen... which would be... $2320."

Abe was staring at Dan. "You can do that kind of math in your head?" he asked.

"Yeah, sorry. I'm kinda freakish with numbers," Dan replied.

"Hmm, good thing," Abe said, and left the surveillance room.

Dan continued watching people entering the casino for most of the rest of the day on the monitors. He spotted five other people doing the same thing he had seen the man and the woman do that morning: come in, go to a machine, discretely insert a payout slip, hit the spin button one or two times, then hit the payout button, get a new payout slip, then head straight for the cashier to cash out, and then leave the casino. He was convinced he was right.

But he was getting very fatigued. Doing this kind of surveillance was much more difficult than the usual casino surveillance work. Normally he could watch different cameras, not have to focus his eyes very hard, and just scan the images for certain predictable behaviors. If he spotted someone winning excessively, then he would zoom in on that person and have to concentrate. Or if he spotted someone acting nervous or trying to hide their movements, then he could follow that person on the camera. But this type of surveillance was different. He had to track as many people as possible as they walked in through the four different entrance doors of the casino, and had to quickly determine where they were headed, following only the ones headed to the slot machines, and try to watch each of those people in their initial moments of play. It was exhausting. He couldn't follow all of them. His eyes ached from concentrating on the four different screens in front of his table. He had many more monitors at his disposal, but he found that he could effectively watch only four screens at one time. He had an hour to go before clocking out. He was just about to call the monitor watching over for the day and head down to the casino floor to just walk around—to give his eyes and brain a rest—when Abe burst back into the surveillance room.

"Dan!" Abe said, "The accountants haven't finished going through all the payout slips from inside the machines, but already they've found eleven slips, each for $175 that are counterfeit. When they run them through the server, there's no machine that generated them."

"Hmmm, okay," was all Dan could say.

"Plus, we've heard back from a couple of the other casinos in town. O'Banion's down the street checks all their payout slips over $100. They've had an average daily loss of $1520 which is like you predicted—sixteen times $95. Pele's Casino checks all their payout slips no matter what the amount, even the ones in the machine, and they're showing no loss. But the Golden Angel has the same policy we do—they check all cashier payout slips of $180 and higher—and they have an average daily $2800 loss over the past three weeks as well."

"Ok," Dan said, so we know it's an organized fraud, consisting of a number of members, and they're hitting multiple casinos in town... and it's probably run by someone who until recently worked inside the casinos, maybe here or maybe at another casino."

"Why someone who used to work?" asked Abe, "Why not someone who still works for a casino?"

"Just a hunch," Dan said. "More of a profile, really. This is someone who, I would guess, got fired or got into some conflict and quit, but someone who is pissed enough to make the kind of effort it would take to pull this off... actually, the profile would be some long-term loyal employee who got passed over for a promotion that he thought he deserved, someone you would never suspect. It's a sophisticated scam, so it has to be someone who knows a lot, someone who's been around long enough to know the different policies of the casinos in town. It doesn't have to be someone who's real computer-savvy... here, look at this." Dan pulled a white slip of paper out of his pocket. "I went down to the floor and put a dollar in a slot machine and played 25 cents and then printed out this payout slip for 75 cents. Look at this piece of paper. It would be fucking easy to counterfeit—it's just some printing with a bar code at the bottom. Looks like a 7-11 receipt. Cheap paper. No encryption. No hard-to-duplicate design. All the cheater would need is an understanding of what was in the bar code and a machine to print them. Hell, he could print the same one over and over. What they really need to do Abe, is link each slot machine to the server, to automatically check each payout slip that's fed into each machine—to verify that another machine connected with the server actually printed that payout slip."

"We don't have that technology," Abe said.

"That technology exists, and it's simple," Dan replied. "It's more a question of whether the casino wants to pay to program all the slots and the server to perform those functions.."

"Well, yeah, you may be right about that."

"I am right, Abe, it's always a question of money. No one wants to spend the money until they get hit big in a fraud. I've seen it time and time again. An ounce of prevention is always too expensive."

"Well... in the meantime, Dan, how do we stop this? How do we catch these people?"

"Stopping them is easy," Dan said. "I can show you how to stop them in one day. But arresting and convicting them is more difficult."

"Say more," Abe said.

"Well, if you merely wanted to stop them, you'd tell the cashiers to notify us every time someone presented a payout slip for $175. We'd detain them, nicely of course, and look at the tape to see what slot machine they had just used. We'd open up that machine and test the most recent payout slip that had been fed into it, which would be the one on the top of the pile in the bin. When that slip turned out to be fraudulent, we'd confront the person with the video evidence and the counterfeit payout slip, confiscate their $175, and tell them never to come back to the casino or they'd be arrested, and then let them go. You wouldn't have to detain and rattle more than three or four of these folks before the leaders of the scam would panic. They'd know the jig was up and wouldn't hit us again... at least not with this particular scam."

"That seems like only a short term solution to the problem," Abe said.

"It is, but it would stop the scam... at least for awhile. On the other hand, if the casino wants to invest in the cure... then they would have to be willing to suffer through a few more days of losing $2800, maybe a week. The issue is building a case that would win in court... that's always the issue..."

Dan paused for a moment. It occurred to him that he had said those very same words to don Fernando back in La Chorrera when he was laying out his plan to trap the murderer they were looking for. Dan quickly shook his head as if to dislodge that memory, and continued talking to Abe. "…that's always the issue. You'd have to dedicate several surveillance officers to monitoring the slots area. We'd have to try and identify the members of this gang, get each of them on tape repeating the same behaviors, and as soon as they leave the slot machine to go to the cashier's window, we'd go over and open up that machine, take out the most recent payout slip they had fed into the machine, dust it for prints, and preserve it… This might be something that would involve the FBI, certainly the Gaming Authority… but we'd have to let the scam continue for enough time until we had enough evidence to arrest the players. And then… then we'd have to confront them with the evidence and get enough of them to flip with a promise of immunity… so that they would testify against whoever was organizing this… yeah, the more I think about it, this is something that's big enough to involve the FBI. It's a federal racketeering charge at least, maybe something that even crosses state lines. But if you got enough of the group to flip, then you could indict the boss. And they would all flip. I've watched five of these folks come in and do this today. They're just low level thieves, most not well dressed, maybe strung out on drugs, not very bright looking. My guess is that whoever is masterminding this is paying them $25 a ticket and keeping $150. And if he's hitting most of the casinos in town… well, these low-lifes are making $100 to $200 a day, and the boss is netting maybe $20,000 a day."

Abe let out a low whistle. "Wow," he said softly.

"Yeah," Dan said. "It's a good scam."

"I've got a meeting with the casino owners in a half an hour," Abe said. "I'll tell them what you said. Hey, and thanks, Dan. This was good work."

"Hey, no problem," Dan said.

"On second thought," Abe added, "how would you like to come to the meeting with me and explain the situation to them yourself? Be a great opportunity to meet the owners."

"Not a fucking chance," said Dan. "I told you when you hired me. I just want a nine-to-five job. No politics. No BS. Just let me do what I do well and go home."

"Are you sure?" Abe asked. "It could lead to a promotion, more money."

Dan looked sternly at Abe and said tersely, "Ask me again and I'll quit."

"Okay, okay. That's a deal. I don't want to lose you. I won't mention anything like that again."

"Okay," Dan said, and turned back to the monitors.

"Thanks, though," Abe said, and then left the room.

Dan hadn't meant to snap at Abe. Abe didn't deserve that. But it was just that memory of saying those same words about building a case to don Fernando that had caused Dan to tense up, to feel angry, on edge. He had wanted to build a case against the Panamanian murder suspect the way he had built so many cases against fraudsters and con men in California: by compiling the evidence piece by piece, layering it in stacks, so that by the time it was presented to a jury, they would be convinced beyond a reasonable doubt that the accused was guilty. Back in the day, he had always prided himself on the fact that prosecutors had never lost a case that he had developed. But it was because he knew the rules of evidence in the U.S. courts... no, that's not right... it was because he *believed in* the rules of evidence, in their efficacy, that he had been so good at building cases... and he had brought that same skill to don Fernando's case against that murder suspect. Dan had been convinced that any Panamanian jury would have found the man guilty...

He tried again to dislodge the thought from his brain. How long did he have to torture himself about this? He did not know—and could not have foreseen— that don Fernando would orchestrate the murder of this suspect. And he couldn't judge don Fernando. That tradition of honor killing was ingrained in his culture. He had talked at length to don Fernando afterwards, and don Fernando simply saw nothing wrong with the tradition. It worked well. The family was vindicated. The transgressor was gone. The public was protected. Lengthy trials and public dismay over the gruesome facts of the suspect's conduct were averted. What was the problem?   And Dan couldn't judge the culture, either. He saw the efficacy of the tradition… he hated to admit it, but he saw it. In a country where the judicial system could be bribed so easily, sometimes only the old traditions made any sense… except… except… except they didn't make any sense to Dan. If it was okay for don Fernando to arrange the murder of a suspect without a trial, then every lynch mob could be justified. Then every tribal stoning of an adulterer was legit. Then mob rule was ok. All of it made Dan sick. It was one thing for Dan to have his own moral code back in the Crenshaw District of L.A. But that personal moral code was useless in another country, another culture where the rules were turned upside down.

Dan looked up at the monitors. What the…? He saw Sara—at least it looked like Sara—enter the casino.

He grabbed the dials of the camera and zoomed in. Yes, it was Sara. Even in the grainy zoom lens, she still looked cute. He pulled the camera back and watched her walk around the casino floor. Ah yes, what a nice looking woman, he thought. What was *she* doing here in the casino?

He switched cameras as she walked from area to area. She didn't seem to have a particular goal—she was just walking around. "Maybe she's just looking," Dan thought to himself, "simply seeing what was in Reno." He followed her as she walked around the blackjack tables, through the slot machine area, and finally up to a craps table. She seemed to position herself there, watching the players and the tosses of the dice. She didn't stand at the table, like she wanted to bet, but stood in the crowd around the table watching the betting. "Nothing unusual about that," Dan thought to himself. "Many gawkers do that." Dan watched as she began talking to a man next to her. A position opened up at the table's rail, and the man moved in to play. Sara moved in with him and they continued to chat. The man put some money down on the table and bought some chips from the dealer. The man put some chips down on the Pass line and continued chatting with Sara. Dan watched as the point was made and the man took odds on the Pass bet and bet the Come line. Sara seemed to be standing closer to the man and they both were chatting more. Dan moved another camera into position and was watching two different camera angles from two different cameras on two different screens in front of him. The man's Come bet made the point and the man took the odds on that and placed another Come bed. Dan watched as the man placed an arm around the small of Sara's back. "Hey, wait a minute," he thought. "They just met," but he noticed that she didn't move away. The man's second Come bet made its point and the man took odds on that. Now the man had three bets on the table, all with odds. Looking at the stack of chips, Dan guessed that the man must have had almost $100 on the table. Dan zoomed the camera closer and counted. Maybe $120. The man placed another Come bet and made that point. Now he had over $150 riding on the table. But the shooter was hot. Dan watched the shooter make five numbers before he crapped out. Dan calculated that the man made a net profit of $200 on his bets. Sara leaned forward and whispered something in the man's ear. The man nodded to Sara and pulled his winnings off the table, and he and Sara headed for the cashier's window.

A dread began to develop in Dan's stomach. He watched the man cash out his chips, and then he followed the man and Sara as they walked, arm in arm, towards the elevators. Dan's shoulders sank, and a terrible sadness filled him. He knew what was about to unfold. The man and Sara got on the elevator and got off on the fifth floor.

The protocol, of course, was that the surveillance officers were supposed to follow all prostitutes to the door of the guest's room and keep the camera positioned on the guest's door until the safety of the guest was ensured. But Dan didn't care about the protocol. He switched the camera to the blackjack table. He didn't even look at the monitor any more. He checked his watch. Close enough to check-out time. He needed to stop at the liquor store tonight. He felt so sad.

Chapter 5

But the next day, Dan didn't have time to think about Sara. The casino owners had called the FBI. When they showed up, Dan had to show them the video recordings and explain how the scam worked. It turned out that the feds were very interested in this case, because they had had reports of similar mysterious losses in casinos up and down the west coast. So the FBI, along with Dan and the other surveillance officers, started tracking the slot machine players, and monitoring the ones who came into the casino with white payout slips in their pockets, laundered them though the slot machines, and cashed out the new slips. Over the next three days, the surveillance team identified a core group of five players who came in regularly twice a day. However, there seemed to be an ever-changing group of about ten or fifteen others who would show up for a couple of days in a row and then disappear. Often times these irregular ones would first appear with one of the core five members. It became clear that the five core members were recruiting and training a ragged group of other cheaters.

There were two FBI agents assigned to Barkley's Casino. Other agents were working with the surveillance officers in Reno's other casinos. Dan watched how the two agents worked—he admired how methodical they were, building their case against each of the cheaters, compiling background reports, collecting old warrants, following the players after they left the casinos to determine where they went to drop off their cash, and where each of them lived. They quickly targeted which one of the players they would make flip—a man named Casey, who had enough prior convictions that one more would send him to prison for at least ten years. The quietly arrested him one morning and had a little "come to Jesus" talk with him. It did not take Casey long to see the light. He agreed to flip, to wear a wire, and, if necessary, to testify in court. From that point on, the case moved quickly. The FBI was able to identify the leader of the conspiracy: a man named Andrew Hightower, who, as Dan had predicted, had been a long-time security officer at O'Banion's Casino, but who had resigned after being passed over for the position of Chief of Security two years ago. He had recruited a group of druggies and hookers whom he had met over the years, and as it turned out, with whom he had been making certain deals over the years—allowing them to practice their trade unhampered at O'Banion's in return for certain favors. After Hightower quit, he recruited them in a revenge plan against the casino, giving them each counterfeit payout slips, instructing them how to use them and how to cash them out. The scam was so successful that he had expanded it to the other casinos in town, and then to casinos in California, Oregon, and Washington.

Hightower and his core group of five would spend about two months in different towns, where they would recruit local druggies and down-and-outs to skim thousands from the local casinos. Then they would move on to the next town, but always return regularly to the Reno area. They had been traveling this circuit for the past two years. Because the daily amount of skim was low—always just below the level that casinos would audit—and because they never stayed more than six to eight weeks in one area, they had gotten away with the scam for two years. The FBI estimated that after paying his team and all the confederates, Hightower himself was pocketing $40,000 a month per casino; and in some towns like Reno, Sacramento, Los Angeles and, of course, Vegas, the team would be targeting four or five casinos a day.

Because of all the tedious video monitoring that the project required, Dan and the other surveillance officers were putting in a lot of overtime. Dan didn't mind that, however. It was a blessed distraction to his memories of that murder in La Chorrera. For once, he felt like the world had some order to it, some justice. On one side, here was a group of druggies and petty criminals doing something they knew was wrong and getting free money they hadn't earned by passing counterfeit payout slips. On the other side, here was a professional pair of FBI agents dispassionately collecting evidence against these criminals—agents who would eventually arrest them and read them their rights. Dan knew that some of these criminals would break down and cry when they realized how much trouble they were in. But that was the nature of accountability. Each of them would have their day in court, before a judge who would weigh the evidence and decide if it was sufficient to bind the defendants over for trial. Each of the defendants could hire a lawyer, and if they couldn't afford one, the state would appoint a lawyer to represent them at no cost. It was a good system, and for those three days, the world made sense to Dan—it was organized into good and evil, but there was a logical process for dealing with it. No matter that this criminal activity was all taking place in a casino—an entire industry that held out the illusion of something for nothing—an industry that depended on human weakness, gullibility, and gambling addiction to keep that income flowing. Dan knew that gambling was foolish, and that an industry that preyed upon human weakness was essentially evil. But, as he had told himself many times in his law enforcement career, two wrongs don't make a right. Robin Hood may have been a folk hero, but he was still a thief, even if the Sheriff of Nottingham was more evil. So Dan worked the overtime willingly, even happily, because something about the project seemed, for those three days, to affirm a sense of right and wrong in his soul. On two of those shifts, he spotted Sara on camera, working the craps table, hooking up with one or two lonely men. But those images didn't bother him anymore. That was simply the way it was.

Finally, when the FBI felt they had enough evidence, they decided to arrest the entire team before the team could leave town. That Thursday afternoon they met with Abe and Dan and three detectives from the Reno police force. The seven of them mapped out a plan to arrest the scam team the next morning. Dan didn't have the authority to arrest anyone outside the casino, so he would remain in the surveillance room and watch for any members of the scam team who might be inside the casino when the arrests went down. Those people he could detain.

That evening, he walked back to the motel feeling wired up, but focused on what would happen tomorrow. He started thinking about a conversation he'd had that afternoon with one of the FBI agents. He had asked the agent to estimate what outcome, what penalty, each of the cheaters might get. The agent explained that the one they were really after was Andrew Hightower—that in terms of the lesser members of the conspiracy, the FBI didn't care if they went to jail or not, so long as they got a felony conviction on their record. But for Hightower, the agent was really hoping for a substantial amount of jail time. The agent went on to explain that, in his opinion, most people could be lured into doing something criminal because most people were weak, but that the act of creating a criminal enterprise—actually thinking up and recruiting people for the counterfeit payout scam—that was much more culpable behavior and more deserving of severe punishment.

"Really?" Dan had said, "So you think there are degrees of evil, some worse than others?"

"Evil?" the agent had replied. "I wasn't thinking of it in terms of evil. I just think he broke more laws, so his punishment should be stronger."

"But don't you think," Dan asked, "that the reason he broke more laws was because he was more evil? I mean, the other folks let themselves be corrupted, but he's the one who corrupted them. Isn't that more evil?"

"I just don't think in those terms," the agent replied, "that word seems... I don't know, old-fashioned."

"Yeah," Dan said, "I suppose it is old-fashioned. But I've always thought that's why we have laws—to define what's evil."

"Hmm," the agent said, "I just think it's to provide order in life. I really don't think much about evil. I just do my job."

That conversation had bothered Dan, but he wasn't sure why, and he pondered it as he walked along. He decided it bothered him on several levels, primarily because he *did* believe in degrees of evil, but secondarily because of the agent's comment about how most people could be convinced to do evil because they were weak. Maybe Dan *was* old-fashioned. Maybe it was his Catholic upbringing. Still, Dan somehow believed in the concept of free will. Maybe that's where he got his concept of degrees of evil as well—from the Church. Because he certainly believed that there were minor sins and major sins, so obviously there had to be degrees of evil. On the other hand, he thought, maybe he was wrong. Maybe doing a little bit of evil was like being a little bit pregnant. Did it matter if the sin was large or small if the person had made the conscious choice to sin? If someone steals from the collection plate, does it matter if he takes one dollar or one hundred dollars? It's still stealing. Of course, Dan thought, the consequences of the larger theft would hurt the church more. Maybe that's why the punishment should be greater for Hightower—because the consequences of his actions were more far-reaching. Maybe the agent was right—that evil had nothing to do with it—that the law punishes consequences instead of the evil nature of the criminal. But Dan was unsatisfied with that line of reasoning. He was unsatisfied with all his ways of thinking about it because they all led to the same conclusion—that he just didn't know. Maybe he should have been a priest rather than a cop, he thought. It was true that he had spent a lot of time thinking about the nature of evil recently, thanks to don Fernando and that fucking murder in La Chorrera. The problem was, he just didn't think of don Fernando as an evil person. In don Fernando's world, he hadn't done anything wrong. Nothing in don Fernando's upbringing, his culture, or his country's laws made an honor killing a sin. It *wasn't* a sin—that was the whole conundrum. It was an *honor* killing. Once the family of the victim made the proper request, don Fernando was honor-bound by his culture, his community, his job, and the law to arrange for that suspect to die. Only Dan thought it was wrong. He couldn't hold don Fernando to blame for it, so he was stuck with a sin that had no sinner. Dan had no name for his own position, either. What do you call it, he asked himself, when there's that a social convention that everyone else in that society thinks is normal, and you're the only one who thinks it's evil? Don Fernando had asked him that very question during one argument they had had after the killing. Don Fernando had gotten mad and shouted, "Who do you think you are, judging us? This is our country, our rules, our community." Dan didn't have an answer to that back then, and he didn't have an answer this evening as he walked back to the motel.

As he was putting his key in his door, Sara's door opened and she stepped out.
"Oh hello, stranger," she said with a smile, "Howya been? Haven't seen you around lately."
"Yeah, well," Dan said, "I've been busy."
"I'm off to meet a friend," she said. "He may have a job for me."
"That's good," Dan said. "What's the job?"
"I'm not quite sure, but it sounds like a runner. You go to all the different casinos and collect these small slot machine winnings that these big gamblers don't have time to collect. My friend says it's all legitimate and I get to keep a percentage of the tickets—in cash!"
Dan felt himself tense up inside. He tried to

keep his voice sounding normal. "Oh yeah? Who's your friend?"

"Just this guy I met. Nice guy. Professional gambler kinda guy," Sara said as she stepped towards her VW bus.

Dan's brain was thinking fast. In another second she would be gone. "Well Sara, you know what they say: if something sounds too good to be true, it usually is. So be careful."

"I will," she laughed, "but I could sure use the cash. See you later." And she was gone.

"Well, fuck me," Dan thought to himself as he stepped inside his motel room. He couldn't risk telling her not to go because if she learned he worked casino security and knew about the scam, she could tip off her friends and the whole arrest process tomorrow would be jeopardized. Fuck! He didn't know her at all— had no idea what kind of person she was. Was she a criminal herself or was she just naïve? Just because she was turning a few tricks at the casino didn't make her a criminal in Dan's eyes. But was she so stupid as to believe that rich gamblers simply don't have time to collect their winnings? Jesus Christ! Anyone who thought it through would see that the story had more holes than Swiss cheese. If they're rich, why are they playing slot machines? If they're playing the slots, and they win, why don't they walk the ten steps to the cashier's window and collect their money? If they're winning at one casino, why would they leave and go to other casinos? Fuck!

Dan thought about it as he drew his bath. He replayed the whole conversation in his head and decided that there was simply nothing else he could have done. Maybe the FBI agent was right; maybe most people are just weak and would do something criminal given the chance.

He let the bath water get extra hot. He needed to not think tonight. He needed to have a drink, soak in the tub, and let the heat and whiskey shut his brain down. And when he was good and relaxed, he could climb out of the tub, cook some dinner and get to bed early.

When the tub was full, he poured himself a glass of whiskey, got undressed, and stepped into the gloriously hot bathtub.

Thirty or forty minutes later, Dan wasn't sure which, he pulled a much more relaxed version of himself out of the water. He slipped into his old bathrobe, poured another drink, threw two hamburger patties into the frying pan, and started cooking dinner.

"Hamburger and cottage cheese", he thought to himself, "I read somewhere that's supposed to be some kind of a diet."

The smell of the cooking hamburger filled the motel room. There's something about the smell of cooking hamburger that is uniquely American—it made Dan feel even more relaxed. When the patties were done, he plopped a scoop of cottage cheese onto a plate with a spoon and then used a spatula to place the patties one on top of the other next to the cottage cheese. Then he added a fair amount of pepper to both the burgers and the cottage cheese and a sprinkle of salt to the burgers. Then he took his plate and his drink and propped himself up in the bed and ate his dinner. It was good.

Chapter 6

The arrests the next morning went down like clockwork, except for Sara's. As part of the tracking procedure over the past three days, the surveillance team had put hidden buttons within reach of every cashier. Whenever a payout ticket within a few dollars of $175 was presented, the cashier would press the button, and someone from the surveillance team would immediately pull the most recent payout slip from inside the slot machine that had been played and check whether it was counterfeit. One of the other security guards had answered a cashier's buzzer, checked the machine, determined that Sara had fed a counterfeit slip into the machine, and had arrested her before she left the casino.

Dan didn't find out about it until Sara was taken to one of the casino's detention rooms. He immediately called Abe.

"Abe, I need a favor." Dan said.

"What is it?"

"Robbie just detained a new dupe, this girl who was passing one of those counterfeit slips for the first time this morning. But I've got reason to believe she was conned into it. This was the first time she's done it." Dan hesitated, then said, "I want permission to cut her free."

There was a pause on the line. "Let me come down and we'll talk," Abe said.

Abe walked into the surveillance room a minute later. He and Dan went into one of the conference rooms and Dan told him what had happened the night before.

"Look Abe, my understanding is that everyone else we've identified has been arrested. The FBI has got strong—very strong—cases against these people. But this girl would be their weakest case. If it wasn't dismissed out of hand, the prosecutor would plead it down to just a misdemeanor. We don't need her—she's small fry. Let's just cut her loose."

Abe pursed his lips, then he asked, "Do you have a personal relationship with her?"

"No. Like I said, I've only spoken to her twice. She just happens to be staying in the same motel as me."

"Not planning on having a relationship with her?" Abe asked.

"Not my type, Abe. She's pretty stupid."

"Some people prefer stupid."

"I don't. Look Abe, the only personal interest I have in this is that I don't want to have to be called to testify. My conversation with her is exculpatory evidence. I knew she was getting conned into this racket and I didn't stop her. I'd be obligated to disclose it to her attorney. He would then call me as a witness as evidence that she was tricked into passing the counterfeit payout slip."

"Exculpatory evidence, huh..." Abe said, rubbing his chin. "A lot of security guards would keep that kind of thing to themselves."

"Yeah, well not me. Look Abe, I'm not saying that I believe she's totally innocent, I'm just saying that it's not worth the effort, and it would be a pain in the ass for me to testify. Plus, once I'm on the witness stand, they could ask me questions about the investigation into the other defendants, what I know, what the FBI said, et cetera. Why risk it?"

Abe was nodding his head, but then he said, "But she did pass a counterfeit slip."

"So confiscate the money, and bar her from the casino."

Abe thought about it some more, then said, "Who arrested her?"

"Robbie," Dan said.

"Ok, wait here a minute," Abe said, then he left the room.

While he was gone, Dan considered what he was doing by asking Abe to let Sara go. Would this damage his relationship with Abe? He was pissed that Sara had put him into this position. But then he realized that she hadn't done that—*he* had chosen to put himself into this situation, and he wasn't sure why. Maybe he was an idiot. Maybe it *was* just because she was cute, just like Abe had intimated. But he wasn't lying to Abe when he said that he believed the case wasn't worth prosecuting.

Abe came back into the room, sat down and said, "Okay, I talked to Robbie. He said the girl is bawling her eyes out, claiming some friend told her the slip was legitimate. I told her to confiscate the money, issue a no-trespassing restraining order against her, and let her go."

"Thanks Abe, I appreciate it."

"Well," Abe said, "I wouldn't have done it for anyone else except you. We wouldn't have uncovered this ring if not for you, so I figured it was a fair trade."

The rest of the day was spent meeting with prosecutors, categorizing the evidence for them, and boxing it up for them. When the police arrested Andrew Hightower, they found his computer and special printer he used to print out the counterfeit payout slips. It was, as they kept telling Abe and Dan, a good bust, a very good bust.

As Dan was clocking out, Abe asked if he would join him for dinner at the buffet. Dan would have preferred his nightly quiet time ritual with a hot bath and a glass of whiskey, but politics was politics, so he accepted the invitation. Besides, Abe offered to pay.

Over dinner, Abe told him how happy the casino owners were with this bust. That part was fine with Dan, but then he felt that Abe was asking questions trying to determine whether Dan would be interested in some type of promotion.

"I appreciate it Abe, but I'm not looking for anything more than what I've got," Dan said.

"Dan, this is a small town," Abe replied. "You could go places."

"The only place I want to go is back to Panama," Dan blurted. Then to explain, he added, "Look Abe, you don't understand. I came back to the states only to get myself together. You advertised this specific job in casino security, which is what I applied for. I like the job, I really do. It suits me. I don't know how long I'll stay. Hell, it may be years. Or not... I don't know. But I'm clear that I don't want to do anything more than what I'm doing. This job is perfect for me. Please, I beg you, don't fuck it up for me."

Abe laughed. "Believe me, Dan, I won't. Hell, I was worried the bosses were going to fire me and give you my job. No, if you're happy, then I'm happy. And anything I can do to increase the chances you'll stay at your job, just let me know."

"No, I'm good. Everything is copacetic."

Of course, everything was not copacetic with Dan. As he walked back to the motel he couldn't help but compare the FBI agents' methodical arrests of all the suspects with his own interference with Sara's arrest. He knew that the FBI agents would have just arrested Sara along with anyone else caught up in their net. Maybe that's what had bothered him about the agent's comment yesterday—that it was "just a job" for them. If Sara passed a counterfeit payout slip, arrest her. Period. No discernment about whether prosecuting a weak case was worth it, both in economic terms and in terms of the emotional stress on a young woman who might in fact have simply been naïve. No moral choice about degree of evil. No application of any personal code of ethics—it was just a job for them. The thought occurred to Dan again that he should have been a priest rather than a cop back in L.A. He had always seen every arrest as a moral choice, not simply a job. There had been many times he had let some criminal act slide, simply because it wasn't "bad enough".

He shook his head as he walked along thinking these thoughts to himself. Maybe the only difference between him and that cop William Grizzard back in the Crenshaw District was just a matter of degree. What was the difference between letting some petty criminal act slide for one suspect and planting evidence on another suspect to strengthen the arrest? Either way, he and William were both making moral decisions on how evil the suspect was and whether or not to intervene in that person's life. Or, for that matter, how was what he had done for Sara that morning any different than what Andrew Hightower had done letting his little gang of drug dealers and hookers ply their trade at O'Banion's? Did he do it because he thought she might be innocent or, as Abe had intimated, was he secretly hoping for some action with her in the future?

Dan had never been this confused about himself before. It was as if the murder in La Chorrera had thrown a huge spotlight on his own code of ethics and exposed every solipsistic crack. Dan didn't necessarily believe in a universal right or wrong, but he had always believed that his personal moral code meant something. He had always lived his life believing that he alone was the arbitrator of what was morally right for him to do in any situation. He had always thought that if he lived his life according to his own personal moral code that somehow he would be exempt from the moral codes of others. But obviously, this was not the case. The thing that had led to his being falsely accused of tipping off that raid in L.A. was that he had been friends with the brother of one of the drug dealers who was being raided. Dan hadn't seen anything wrong with being friends with someone whose brother was a dealer. The thing that had led don Fernando to assume Dan wouldn't freak out about the murder was that he and don Fernando had done a few profitable, but technically illegal, projects together around the cities of Villa Rosario and La Chorrera. Dan hadn't seen anything wrong with a little corruption. Minor corruption was the norm in Panama, and Dan had no problem with that. But honor killing was something else entirely, at least it was to Dan. And he had no one to blame for it except himself and his own belief that he could navigate the slippery slope of a few minor illegal projects with don Fernando. What, he wondered, what was the value in having a moral code if everyone else in your world operated in a different moral code that could overwhelm your own code? And if that was true, what *was* a moral code? Just an excuse to do what you wanted? Was a personal moral code even possible? Dan just didn't know anymore.

As he walked past the motel office and stepped into the parking lot, he saw Sara loading up her VW bus. It looked like she was moving out. That didn't surprise him.

"I just had the worst day of my life!" she exclaimed when she saw him.

Dan was tired. He really didn't want to talk with her, but he didn't want to be unkind.

"Oh?" he said.

"Yeah, I got fucking arrested at that fucking Barkley's casino! They held me in a room in handcuffs for over an hour until I finally convinced them I was innocent and they let me go. I told them I hadn't done anything wrong! My friend Dwayne gave me a slot machine ticket to cash out for him. Those fucking guards said it was counterfeit! As soon as they let me go, I raced over to Dwayne's house, but they had arrested him, too. This town is fucked! I'm going back to Sacramento."

She slammed the door of her VW van and then opened it again. "Dwayne gave me a whole stack of slot machine tickets last night—they're probably all counterfeit! He told me to only cash two a day. Now I know why. That fucking asshole!"

Dan couldn't help himself. He asked, "It didn't strike you as suspicious that someone you just met would give you a stack of payout slips and tell you to only cash two a day?"

Sara stopped, looked at Dan, and took a deep

breath. He watched her eyes move left and right, as if she was thinking. Then she said, "No... well, yeah... yeah, it did seem odd... but he kept saying they were legitimate."

"In my experience, Sara, when someone keeps insisting that something is legitimate, it usually means it's not," Dan said.

"Yeah, you're fucking right about that. Well, I gotta finish packing," she said and walked back into her room.

Dan unlocked his door and went inside. He immediately poured himself a drink, stretched out on the bed, and tried to clear his mind.

A minute later, there was a knock on his door. He got up, drink in hand, and opened it. It was Sara. She was holding a stack of slot machine payout slips.

"You wouldn't be interested in buying these, would you?" she asked. "I'd give you a real good price."

Dan looked at her. What a pretty face. Why was it that a pretty girl could get away with being so stupid?

"No Sara, not on your life," he said. Then he added, "I don't want to get arrested, either."

She frowned. "Yeah, you're probably right. But I sure could have used the money Dwayne promised me." Then her face lit up, as if some good idea had just occurred to her. "Hey," she said to Dan, "you wouldn't be interested in partying, would you? I'd make you a good deal on that too."

"No, Sara, thanks, but not tonight. I'm very tired. You have a safe drive to Sacramento."

Sara looked glum, but nodded her head. "Yeah... man oh man, this just hasn't been my day."

"Well, look at the bright side, Sara," Dan said. "The casino let you go, didn't they? You dodged that bullet. You're not in jail like your good buddy Dwayne."

"Yeah, that's true," she replied. "Well, I gotta go pay my bill, and then I'd better get going. You take care now." And she turned and walked toward the office.

"You too," Dan said, as she walked away.

Dan went back inside, closed the door and stretched back out on the bed and took another sip of whiskey. A minute or two later he heard the door of Sara's VW bus open and shut and the motor start up, and the sound of it pulling away. In a minute, he thought, I'll run the tub. Then all will be well. But then there was another knock on the door.

"Jesus," he said under his breath, and once again got up from the bed, holding his drink, and opened the door. The night clerk, a young guy named Mitch, was standing there. He was holding several payout slips in his hand.

"Sorry to bother you, Mr. Landes, but you know that girl who was in the room next to yours?"

"Yeah."

"Well she just checked out, and she told me she didn't have time to cash in her winning slot machine tickets, and so she gave these to me to pay for her room. But I got to thinking a minute ago, that maybe I shouldn't have accepted them. She said she didn't have time—that her brother was sick in Sacramento and she had to get home right away."

"Uh, huh," Dan said.

"Well, sir, I know you work at Barkley's and I wonder if you could look at them and tell me if they're real."

"I don't need to look at them, Mitch. They're counterfeit," Dan said. "We just busted a bunch of people today for passing them. It'll be in the paper tomorrow."

"Oh damn... damn damn fuck!" Mitch said. "I'm going to get fired for sure."

Mitch looked around. He looked like he was about to cry. "Damn," he said again, and then he looked at Dan and asked, "What should I do, Mr. Landes?"

Dan thought for a moment. Mitch was a nice kid, probably more decent than Sara. "Well, I can't tell you what to do, Mitch. But if it were me, I'd just claim the girl booked without paying. In a way that's kind of true."

Mitch's eyes lit up. "Yeah, yeah…" he said, then he looked at Dan. "You won't rat me out, will you, Mr. Landes?"

Dan shook his head no. "No, I won't, Mitch. But I will give you one piece of advice. If you try to use those slot machine slips, you *will* be arrested. I guaran-damn-tee it."

Mitch's eyes widened and he looked at the slips in his hand like they were poison ivy. "Yes, sir, Mr. Landes. Thank you, sir."

"Goodnight Mitch," Dan said and closed his door.

Dan went into the bathroom and turned the tub's hot water on. "What a fucking day," he thought to himself.

Chapter 7

After the arrests for the counterfeit payout slips, almost all the Reno casinos began retrofitting their slot machines with a computer program that connected them to the casinos' servers. The servers instantaneously verified that every payout slip fed into the machine by a player corresponded to the data from whatever slot machine had printed that slip. Of course, Dan assumed it would just be a matter of time before someone figured out a way around that. But for the moment, it would prevent that particular scam. So for a few weeks, things were quiet, and work seemed to take on a comfortable routine. Abe said that this was a normal pattern—that whenever there was a big bust at a casino, all the other crooks, cheaters, and con artists in town would lay low for a while, worried that casino security was still hyper-vigilant. Whatever the reason, Dan was happy for the lull.

And those few weeks were relatively quiet at Sheila's Inn, too. There was, of course, the continual rotation of "guests" at the motel, and the occasional rowdy party when someone actually won a little money at the casinos, usually followed by several quiet drunken evenings with the curtains drawn after the guest went back to the casinos and lost all his winnings—and more—over the subsequent days.

The infrequent parties were rarely a problem. Sheila's used a security service shared by several of the motels on that side of town. The night clerk only had to call them if some party got out of hand. Dan liked that. After spending all day in an environment of clanging bells and the continuous babble and yelling of the casino soundtrack, he just wanted to come back to his room after work and enjoy silence. There was both a television and a radio in the room, but Dan never turned them on. He found the silence very healing—the silence, the hot baths and, of course, the whiskey.

But that's the dilemma with any routine. We yearn for it when there is too much chaos, but when there's too much routine, we get bored and yearn for something—anything—exciting… something to "break the routine"… which is how Dan ended up going bowling with Ashley.

It was the end of Dan's shift on a Tuesday. It hadn't been a bad day, but it hadn't been a particularly interesting one, either. Tuesdays were always the slowest days in any Reno casino/hotel. The weekend partiers had all left Monday. The Wednesday night "special promotion" crowd wouldn't check in until the next afternoon, and the next weekend crowd wouldn't start filtering in until Thursday afternoon. The only thing of interest on this particular Tuesday was that Dan and Robbie had spent about thirty minutes watching a blackjack player who was winning relatively consistently. It was not a lot of money, just steady good hands. But after surveilling him and the dealer for a while, both Dan and Robbie concluded he was just on a small winning streak, and they turned their attention to scanning the floor for pickpockets. When the clock finally read 5:00 p.m., Dan punched out and was walking through the casino floor towards the exit, wondering if he shouldn't do something that evening before heading to the motel. He had eaten a late lunch, so he wasn't hungry; but he was thinking about having a drink. He was considering stopping at some bar and just having a few beers. But before he got to the casino exit, he ran into Ashley. She obviously had just clocked out from her job as a barback and was headed toward the same exit.

"Hey, Ashley," he said. "How's it going?"

"It's good now," she said. "But it was a slow day."

"Yeah," Dan replied, "that it was."

They both were walking side by side toward the exit when suddenly Ashley stopped, looked at Dan, and asked, "Hey, Dan, do you bowl?"

"Not in months with an 'R' in them," Dan replied.

"No, seriously, do you know how to keep score in bowling?"

"Seriously? Well, um, it's been years, maybe decades, but I certainly have done it," Dan said.

"My bowling team has a tournament tonight, like in thirty minutes, and our scorekeeper has pimped out on us. Would you be willing to come and keep score for us?" she asked.

Visions of a hot bath and whiskey on ice were being threatened in Dan's mind.

"Um, hmmm, weeelll..." he started to say.

"It's at the bowling stadium," she said. "A two minute walk."

"Hmmm..."

"I'll pay for all your drinks," she pleaded.

"Really? You can drink there?" he asked

"Of course! Come on, we really need a scorekeeper. The tournament rules say no team member can keep score—it has to be an outsider. Pleeease?"

A few days later, when Dan was thinking back and reconstructing the conversation, he wondered exactly why he said yes. Of course, he knew that casino's security staff were forbidden to fraternize with other casino employees—it was a rule that was supposed to prevent conspiracies and employee theft—but he simply didn't believe in that rule, so he ignored it. He may have said yes because she happened to ask him just as he was thinking about doing something—anything— different on his way home to the motel; it may have been because she was pretty; it may have been because she was pleading with him so sweetly; it may have been because of the promise of free drinks; or it may have been because he had nothing else to do and was willing to help out a friend. But he decided it probably was because she was pretty. It certainly was not because he liked bowling, and most certainly not because he was drawn to the idea of going to a large loud entertainment center with crashing pins and rolling balls and people shouting and creating the same din as the casino he was trying to walk out of. No, it was because she was pretty. And so he said "Okay, I'll do it" in a more upbeat voice than he felt, but then he added, "but don't keep me out too late—I'm an old man, you know."

"Not *that* old," Ashley laughed. "Come on, let's go."

As they walked through the Reno streets on the way to the bowling stadium, Dan asked her about her bowling team.

"I didn't know you were on a bowling team," he said.

"Actually, I'm the team captain. Our team has won two state championships."

"Really?" Dan said.

"Bowling is a huge deal in Reno, Dan," Ashley explained. "If you don't gamble—and a lot of the locals don't—then you bowl. It's the only other thing to do in town."

"Huh, I didn't know that," Dan said. "Although, I had noticed that there wasn't much to do around here. At first I thought it was just a distorted view because of the nature of my job. You know, all I ever see is people either gambling or drinking. But after the last few weeks here, I concluded those *were* the only two choices in town."

"Ha," Ashley laughed. "You oughta take up bowling. It's lots of fun, and great exercise."

"Uh huh… is there a geriatric league?" Dan asked.

"Yeah, actually there is, but they have strict rules and you're too young for it. Plus, they're damn good. Fucking good. Cutthroat good."

Dan laughed. The idea of cutthroat senior bowlers seemed funny.

"It's true," Ashley said. "They'll 'accidentally' step on your foot with their walkers just to hamper your game."

Dan laughed again. He liked Ashley's sense

of humor. It was glib without being mean. And he discovered that he liked watching her bowl, too. He had only seen her working the bar, busing the tables, or cleaning glasses. But now he got to watch her doing an activity she loved, and she moved like a cat in that bowling alley—smooth and fluid, totally concentrating on those pins, winding up and letting that bowling ball sail down the lane towards them. Those pins didn't stand a chance, Dan thought.

Dan also discovered what a fast-paced game it was. As the scorekeeper, he had to concentrate on every player, and every throw. What made it difficult was that Ashley had told one of the servers to keep Dan's beer glass full, and that particular server took Ashley at her word. And while Dan had had a late lunch, he was basically drinking on an empty stomach. But he managed to keep score and not make any math errors.

Ashley's team was the Reno Rockets, an all-girl team, and they were pitted against the Delta Rollers, another all-girl team. Dan didn't get the name of the league. But based on the number of strikes he saw, he guessed it was a semi-professional league. They were playing best-of-three matches for advancement in some kind of seasonal tournament. Dan didn't really care about that, but he did notice how competitive and determined both teams were. He also guessed, based on the appearance of many of the women, and the amount of hugging and touching that seemed to occur within each team every time someone scored a strike, that many of the team members were lesbians. While that was of no concern to him one way or the other, he did wonder if that was true for Ashley.

He got his answer, or at least a partial answer, later that evening. The Rockets won the first two games, which meant that a third game wasn't required. Normally, the Rockets would go out and celebrate after a win. But it was a Tuesday night and all three of Ashley's teammates had to work the next day. Ashley, however, had Wednesday off, and she was still excited about her team winning, and the evening was still young. So she asked Dan if he wanted to get a bite to eat with her to celebrate the victory. And so, for the second time that evening, he accepted her invitation. Her being pretty had something to do with that as well, but it was more because by now Dan was very hungry.

"My only request is that we go somewhere quiet," Dan said as they left the bowling stadium.

"There's Terri's, by the river," Ashley suggested, "it's always quiet, and they've got pretty good burgers.

"Sounds good," Dan said. "Lead the way."

As they walked through downtown, Dan asked her one question about how she got to be captain of the team, and Ashley bubbled over with the history of the Rockets, who had formed them, when she joined, the rivalries, the victories, the defeats, and how she had worked her way up to captain last year. Dan listened quietly and smiled. He liked her enthusiasm. He didn't have any of that in his life. It was nice to be around that kind of excitement.

They got to the restaurant, ordered food and drinks at the counter and sat down at a corner table to wait.

"Sorry I was babbling on so much," she said. "We really needed that win tonight. If we win the next game, we'll be in the semi-finals."

"No, I enjoyed listening to you," Dan said. "It's a different world from what I'm used to."

"So, what brought you to Reno?" Ashley asked.

"Oh, that's a long story," Dan said. "I mean, the short answer is the job. I just needed some place in the states to rest for awhile, just to 'get my head together' as they used to say."

"What do you mean 'in the states'? Where were you living before?" Ashley asked.

"I've spent the last ten years in Panama."

"Really? How cool!" Ashley exclaimed. "Do you speak Spanish and all?"

"Yeah, pretty much. Learned it in high school."

"Why did you leave?"

"Well, I guess *that's* the long story." Dan paused. He wasn't sure he wanted to explain, but somehow the words came out of him anyway. "You know I used to be a detective in California?"

"Yeah, I had heard that," Ashley said.

"Well, I quit that job and moved to Panama about ten or eleven years ago, and I really liked it... I still like it. It's a beautiful country... wonderful country. But this past year, I kind of got... drawn into a murder case down there, and, well... I guess it kind of freaked me out. I only did white-collar crime investigations in California. I was never involved with any of the violent crime cases unless they needed help analyzing a suspect's computer hard drive or something. Anyway, I was friends with some of the police down in Panama, and they asked me to help out on this murder investigation and I ended up seeing some violent stuff there that... well, it disturbed me... and I just needed to get away for awhile and think it through."

"Yeah," Ashley said softly. "Violence sucks."

"My work in California was all white-collar, you know, scams, embezzlements, frauds, tax evasion, money laundering... that kind of shit," Dan explained. "And I viewed crime as a kind of game. I thought that all people committed crimes because of the lure of easy money. I thought that *they thought* it was a game, you know, like the way these high rollers come to the casino thinking they can somehow beat the odds. I was naïve, I guess... but I understood those people. I understood how they thought, what made them tick. But in Panama, I saw a different side of evil. And I realized I didn't understand people at all. So I decided to take a vacation, so to speak... come back to the states for awhile. I've still got my apartment in Panama. I figured I would stay here for awhile, and go back when I figured it out."

"Figured it out?" Ashley asked, "What's the it?"

Dan paused. "Well, I don't know, exactly. I think

the thing I'm trying to figure out... and this will sound strange... but I think it's the nature of evil. I mean, I understand people who cheat, who scam, who con others... I've talked to so many of them over the years, and they all admit that what they do is wrong—they *know* it's wrong, but they do it anyway... but I don't understand people who do violence, real violence, to other human beings, and then simply don't see it as wrong. I just don't get that."

Ashley was listening quietly, looking at Dan and nodding her head.

"Anyway," Dan said, "that's a long answer to a short question. What about you? What brought you to Reno? It wasn't the bowling, was it?"

Ashley looked away. "No. I was working in Vegas, living with this guy, and well, it kind of turned into a... a domestic violence situation. He ended up going to jail for a month. When he got out, we got back together...." She gave a half-smirk when she saw Dan's frown. "Yeah, I know that was stupid, but I thought I loved him... and then it happened again, and he beat me up pretty bad the second time. He had a bad drinking problem. They put him back in jail for six months. I decided to move out of Vegas. I didn't want to be there when he got out of jail."

"I'm sorry, Ashley," Dan said.

She shrugged. "It was my own damn fault. All my friends warned me. Anyway, that was three years ago. When I got here, I was kind of lost, and I got into the bowling thing by accident, but I threw myself into the game, just because when I'm bowling, I'm not thinking about him. It's a very intense game, you know."

"Yeah, I never thought of bowling that way before," Dan said, "but I saw that tonight."

"Oh yeah, those women are very competitive, but they've become my best friends here."

"And what happened to that guy?"

"I don't know. After the second fight, I cut off all contact with him. I hope I never see him again. I really don't know what I'd do if he showed up, you know. It was so weird, after the first fight, when I went back to him.... My friends in Vegas all said I was crazy... but he said he was sorry; he said he would change; but he didn't... and yet I stayed, and I knew, I *knew* he hadn't changed... but there was something about him.... At the time, I told myself it was love, you know, all that shit about how love is difficult, about how you have to work at it—I believed that shit! But I don't think love should be that much work. When I first got to Reno, I was seeing a therapist for a while, and she told me it wasn't love I had for him—it was an addiction. That opened my eyes. The more I looked at it that way, the better I felt about myself... because, you know, I thought it was all my fault... that it was *my fault* he went to jail... my fault he lost his job... shit! I was cray-cray."

The waiter came over to the table with their food. While they were eating, Dan said, "I have this theory about some people. I think that some people are like the La Brea Tar Pits. You know what the La Brea Tar Pits are?"

Ashley mouth was full of hamburger, but she shook her head no.

"They are these huge natural tar pits in one area of Los Angeles," Dan explained. "Been there for thousands of years. Dinosaurs used to step into them and get stuck. They're like quicksand. Once the dinosaurs stepped into them, they couldn't pull themselves out and they were slowly sucked underneath, and died. They're famous because scientists keep finding these really well-preserved dinosaur bones in them. Anyway, the city put this huge iron fence around them to keep people from stepping into them and getting stuck."

Ashley swallowed her food and asked, "Why would people step into them? Couldn't they just see them?" Ashley asked.

"No, that's the point," Dan said. "They're black tar, but when they get covered by dust, dirt, and leaves, it just looks like normal ground. Same reason people get caught in quicksand—the ground looks normal until you're sinking, and then you can't extricate yourself because you're in too deep. Well, my theory is that some people are like those tar pits. They look normal, but once you've stepped into their lives, they're like tar pits, and it's really tough to pull out of the relationship; they're always sucking you in, deeper and deeper. And the only way to deal with them—the only way!—is to build a fence around them, to never see them or talk to them, because you can't touch them..." Dan paused. "It's just my own theory, but I've found that the only way to protect myself from those kinds of people is to build a fence, a huge iron fence, all around them. Nothing else works."

"I like that theory," Ashley said.

"Yeah, well, it took me years to figure it out," Dan said. "You know," he added, "you were right—these really are good burgers."

Ashley smiled. "Aren't they? Best in town, I think."

Dan and Ashley sat at that table at Terri's for almost two hours, drinking beer and just talking. Dan was amazed how easy it was to just talk and laugh with her. Finally, he pointed out the hour.

"I know you have tomorrow off, Ashley, but I have to work."

"Understood," she said, and stood up.

They paid their bill and walked out of the restaurant and started walking back towards Barkley's. Dan realized he didn't know where Ashley lived, or whether she had driven to the casino and left her car there. He was a little concerned because they both had drunk a number of beers.

"Uh," he said, "I don't mean to be nosy, but where do you live? You're not driving home from the casino, are you?"

"Oh no," she laughed, "I walk to work. I live in the Balboa Apartments. You know, the big orange building?

We passed it on the way here.”

“Oh yeah, I looked at them when I first came to town,” Dan said. “They were okay, but it was cheaper for me to stay at the motel.”

“Yeah, well, I had all my furniture when I got here,” Ashley said.

“Yeah, that makes sense,” Dan said.

They walked and chatted up to the Balboa, where Ashley gave him a hug. “Thanks for helping us out tonight,” she said.

“I enjoyed it, Ashley. I had a really good time tonight. Thanks for inviting me.”

“I had a good time too,” Ashley said, “I was lucky to run into you tonight. Maybe you can keep score for us again sometime.”

“Any time,” Dan said. Ashley gave him another quick hug, and turned and walked into the apartment building. Dan watched until she was safely inside, then started heading towards his motel.

“Hmm,” he thought to himself. “What a strange turn of events. Who would have thunk it?”

Chapter 8

A few days later, Robbie called Dan over to his set of video monitors. Robbie had been watching the blackjack tables.

"Hey Dan, come over here a sec, would you? Our friend is back," he said.

"Which one?" Dan asked.

"That player from a few days ago, remember him?" Robbie said and zoomed in one of the cameras so that Dan could see the player's face.

"Oh yeah, that guy," Dan said. "I remember him. He was winning."

"Well, he's winning again. I've been watching him for the last hour. He's not winning all the time, but overall, he's always ahead."

"Maybe he's just a good player," Dan said.

"Well, no, actually, he's a really bad player. That's what I can't figure out. There's no method to his playing, but he wins more than he loses. Here, look at this." Robbie rewound the digital recording. "See here, the dealer has dealt him two fours, and watch! He splits them. No one splits fours. But he does, and watch... See, he wins both hands. And watch this," Robbie said as he fast-forwarded the recording. "Here he's got a nineteen, and he hits! Who hits on a nineteen? But he pulls a two against the dealer's twenty, and wins. His playing makes no sense, but he's winning. I think something's up. I just can't figure out what it is."

"Yeah?"

"He's got some advantage, but I just can't see it," Robbie said. "The only thing I notice is that he's sitting at first base again, closest to the shoe, just like he was the other day."

"What cameras are on that table?" Dan asked

"39 through 44," Robbie said.

"Ok, let me watch him for awhile. You take over the slots area," Dan said. Dan went back to his console and pulled up those cameras. He angled one camera to look directly down on the table in front of the man, so Dan could watch both the cards and the player's hands. There were no unusual hand movements. The man never touched the cards. The dealer would deal the players one card each, all face up, and then deal himself one card face up, then deal each player their second card, also face up. Finally, the dealer dealt himself his second card, face down. Then the betting would start, starting with the player that Dan was watching. He would either hit or stand, sometimes double-down or split, sometimes not. Sometimes he took insurance; sometimes he didn't. Robbie was right—there was no method to his playing—no consistency—but he won more than he lost. And that's what made it weird. Most of the players who came to Reno really had no idea how to gamble. They would play hunches or "systems" they had read about, and occasionally they might win a hand or two. But over the long run, they would lose. The house edge was against them, doubly against them if they played poorly, because math is a harsh teacher. But this guy kept winning. Not a lot, but more than probability said he should be.

After about thirty minutes, Robbie rolled his chair over to Dan's console.

"Whaddya think?" he asked Dan.

"Well, I agree with you. Something's up," Dan said.

"He's not a counter," Robbie said, "because he never increases his bets. Plus he'll chat away with the cocktail waitresses or other players until it's his turn to bet. And he doesn't seem to ever look at what anyone else's cards are."

"Yeah, I saw that," Dan said. "But there is some kind of pattern here. I can feel it. Listen, I'm going to just sit here and look for patterns. Why don't you go down to the floor and watch him for twenty minutes or so, and then come up and let's talk."

"Okay," Robbie said, and got up.

Dan watched the betting some more. Then he opened up the table camera on one of his screens—a small camera on the blackjack table that could give a full screen view of any player's face. Dan focused it on this man, and kept his other monitor looking down on the table showing the cards. Dan studied the man's face. He was about 65 years old, with a round face and a thin, slightly hooked nose and an olive complexion... maybe Italian, Croatian, or possibly Argentinean... Dan couldn't quite place the features. It was a pleasant enough face... relaxed, not stressed, the kind of person you would pass on the street, notice, and promptly forget... friendly, but undistinguishable. His hair was black, probably dyed, but thinning. His clothes were nice, but not expensive. Just a face in the crowd. Dan watched his eyes. Robbie was right—he wasn't a card counter. He never even glanced at the cards that the other players received. Dan watched his eyes closer, then Dan watched the other monitor. What the...? Dan watched another ten minutes of play, going back and forth between the two monitors every time it was the man's turn to bet. Dan started putting electronic markers on both recordings every time it was the man's choice to hit or stand.

After twenty minutes Robbie came back up into the surveillance room.

"I couldn't see anything unusual," Robbie said. "He's just a bad player who keeps winning. Did you have any luck?"

"Yeah, I think so," said Dan. "I thought there was a pattern, you know, something that he was doing, but I finally realized it was something he wasn't doing, Robbie. He never busts. No matter what hand he's dealt, he never takes a bust card. He may lose to the dealer's better hand, but he never loses by busting."

"Really?" Robbie said, and pulled his chair up beside Dan to look at the monitor.

"Yeah, here... look," Dan said and rewound the recording. "Here he has a twelve, and the dealer is showing a nine. Anyone who's knows basic betting strategy would hit the twelve. But he doesn't—he stands. But look, the next player takes a card, and it's a ten. If our guy had hit, he would have busted. And look at this—I marked the tape every time it was his turn to bet. Watch both monitors and watch his eyes when it's his turn."

Dan fast-forwarded the recording to four different times when it was the man's turn to bet.

"He looks at the shoe," Robbie said under his breath.

"Right," Dan said, "and that's the only time he ever looks at the shoe."

"You think it's a marked deck?" Robbie asked.

"I don't know. I mean, *he's* not marking it. I watch his hands—he never touches the deck. Maybe he's got an accomplice—another player—who's marking the deck.... Who's this dealer?"

"That's Brad," said Robbie.

"Is he new?"

"No, he's worked here a few years. We've had no problem with him," Robbie said.

Dan picked up the telephone and called the pit boss and asked him to have the floor manager rotate Brad off that table, put another dealer there, open up six new decks of cards for that table, and to save the old cards for inspection. He hung up the phone and he and Robbie watched on the monitor as a new dealer took over that table, placed six new decks in the automatic shuffler, then placed them in the shoe, burned the first card, and started dealing out hands. The player seemed unperturbed by the break, and simply ordered a fresh cup of coffee from the cocktail waitress and chatted with another player. When it came time to bet, the player continued as he had been before, betting the same amount each time, hitting or standing in random ways, but never busting, and only losing when the dealer had a better hand. Dan and Robbie started keeping track of what card the player sitting next to him received after the man stood pat—in every case it was the same: if the man would have taken that next card, he would have busted.

"That's how he's winning, Robbie," Dan said. "He's eliminated his chances of busting. The dealer might get a better hand and beat him, but this guy will never lose by busting himself. That's what creates the house edge, you know, the fact that the player has to go first. Even with a 12, a player has a bust rate of thirty-one percent if he hits, and it goes up dramatically from there. This guy has simply eliminated all the losses that come from the possibility of busting. He doesn't have to count cards—he wins by not busting."

"You want me to get a no trespassing order against him?" Robbie asked.

"No, not yet. I want to figure out how he does it first. We don't know who else might be involved. And that's another odd thing. If I had a good system at blackjack, I'd be playing the high roller tables, not this little five-dollar minimum table. I mean, I've calculated he's only won two hundred so far, and he's been playing for, what? Two or three hours?"

"Yeah, that is weird," Robbie said. "Maybe he's still practicing, working out the kinks with the con, or maybe training a partner."

"Yeah... let's just watch him and record all his play time. Oh, and hey, let's find out if he's using a Players Club card, too."

Just then, there was a knock on the door. Robbie answered it. It was the pit boss with a small cardboard box holding the cards that Brad had been dealing at that table. Dan heard the pit boss ask Robbie if Brad was under any suspicion.

Dan interjected from across the room, "No, not at all. This has got nothing to do with him. He's clean."

"That's good," the pit boss said. He's a good dealer. I don't want to lose him."

"No, he's okay," Dan said. "Hey, is the player at first base using a Players Club card?"

"I'll check," the pit boss said.

"Thanks."

After the pit boss left, Robbie asked Dan how he knew that Brad wasn't involved.

"I don't know how I know that. It's just a feeling," was all Dan could say.

Dan and Robbie watched the man play for another hour before he took his winnings to the cashier's window and left the casino.

Dan called down to that particular cashier and asked how much she had paid him. It was $325.

"Have you ever seen that guy here before?" Dan asked Robbie.

"No, never. Not before—what was it?—two days ago, when we first watched him?"

"Hmm, okay. Well, I don't want to spook him," Dan said. "I snapped a picture of his face, but let's wait to see if he returns before we circulate that to the other casinos. In the meantime, let's look at those cards."

Dan and Robbie each put on latex gloves and started examining the cards. The cards had the appearance of the casino's brand. They examined the edges for crimping, but found none. They felt the backs of the cards for pinpricks or blistering, but felt nothing. They found no shadings, daub marks, scraped areas or shavings on the cards. They placed the backs of the cards under ultraviolet and infrared light, but found no inks or dyes. They placed several of the cards under a video microscope and examined the magnified backs of the cards on a special computer screen, looking for any indication that the cards were marked. They found none. They examined the boxes the cards came in, to ensure they were manufactured at the correct facility. They ran the serial numbers from the boxes against the purchase orders. Everything checked out—the cards did not appear to have been tampered with in any way.

The phone rang. It was the pit boss with the customer's Players Club card information. Dan wrote down the name, Michel Diego, and his Players Club ID number. Okay, Dan thought, he's not Italian or Croatian after all—he's Hispanic.

"That's odd," Dan said to Robbie as he hung up the phone.

"What's that?"

"Well, the guy used a Players Club card. You know, con men usually won't do that. They don't want to be identified."

"Maybe he's new at this racket," Robbie offered.

"Or maybe we're wrong, and he's just an incredibly lucky player. Well, that's another reason not to do anything until we watch him some more, assuming we ever see him again. In the meanwhile, let's look at Mr. Diego's Players Club application.

Dan went to their data computer and typed in the man's name and Players Club ID number. A copy of Michel Diego's original application for his Players Club card appeared on the screen, along with a copy of his driver's license and a history of every time he'd played at Barkley's. Dan printed out copies of all three documents and took them back to his desk to study them.

"He's from Uruguay," Dan said out loud. "Well, I was kind of close... Applied for his card last year... but he's only been here a few times... Nothing much here, Robbie."

"I'll have the police do a criminal records check," Robbie said.

"Okay," Dan said, "but I bet it won't show anything."

Dan pulled the photo he had taken of the man's face up on his computer screen and looked at it carefully. He didn't particularly recognize the face, but there was this nagging feeling of having seen it, or someone similar, before. He pulled up the recording that he had taken the photo from, and just watched the man's face in motion. His face was relaxed, almost friendly, with just the hint of a smile. It was only when it came his turn to bet that—just for a microsecond—his eyes would steel up and glance quickly at the shoe and then at his cards. Dan could almost see the man doing the math in his head, and then his eyes would relax, and he would signal to the dealer whether he wanted another card or not. It was only in that quick glance at the shoe that his face changed at all, and even then the change was only in his eyes. But it was those eyes... Dan felt he knew that look, as if he had seen someone else do that microsecond tell—that quick cold steely look—but Dan couldn't remember who or when. He slowed the recording down, frame by frame, until the frame where the man shifted his gaze and looked at the shoe. Then Dan hit the pause button and just looked at the man's eyes. He zoomed in a bit on the image and looked at the man's pupils. He hadn't noticed it before, but they seemed slightly dilated. That was odd, because the casino was well lit. Dan wondered if it was a medical condition... or maybe he had just come from having his eyes checked and the optometrist put those drops in... Maybe that's why his glance at the shoe seemed so steely and stern—maybe he was having trouble seeing.

He picked up the phone and called the pit boss. "Hey, it's Dan upstairs," he said. "Can you do me a favor and close that table? Thanks."

Dan hung up the phone and said to Robbie, "I'm going down to examine that shoe and the table. Can you pull the tape of this guy from the other day and just fast-forward through it and make a rough estimate of how much he won?"

"Will do," Robbie said.

As he walked downstairs Dan began to have second thoughts. It wasn't unusual for someone to win $300 at a blackjack table on a lucky session. There was nothing about this guy's conduct at the table that was unusual—for a typical bad player, that is. Maybe Dan was just barking up the wrong tree. The laws of probability are only laws in the long run. In the short run, they're just odds. Maybe the guy was just lucky. Still, those eyes were interesting.

Dan got to the table and picked up the shoe and examined it carefully. Nothing seemed amiss. He felt the table in front of, and around, where the shoe had been placed. He bent down and looked underneath the table and felt the underneath side with his fingers. He wasn't sure what he was looking for—maybe some kind of apparatus, or device—but he found nothing.

The pit boss came over and said to Dan, "Anything I should know about?"

"No, not really," Dan said, and then he laughed. "You know how suspicious we get when someone wins a little money."

The pit boss nodded his head. "Yeah, I saw that guy. Crappy player. But just lucky."

"Yup," Dan said. "Well, everything looks in order. The cards were clean. The table's clean. We didn't see anything in the videos."

"You guys watch everything," the pit boss commented. "Even the minor winners."

"Yeah... well..." Dan started to say.

"No," the pit boss interrupted. "I mean that in a good way. All the dealers know that. And it keeps everyone honest."

"Except the cheaters," Dan chuckled.

"Except the cheaters," the pit boss repeated.

Dan went back upstairs. Part of him wanted to just forget this Diego fellow. He had only won a small amount. There were no signs of any cheating. There wasn't even anything Dan could investigate as odd—except for the fact that he never busted his cards. This wasn't even a case Dan could talk to Abe about—there simply was nothing there.

Still, when he got back up to his console, he pulled up the recordings again. Dan decided to ignore the overhead camera and the face camera, and just watch one of the other views, one that was focused not directly on Diego but at a downward angle. "I'll just watch fifteen minutes more," Dan told himself. He rewound the recording to the point just after the pit boss switched Brad off the table. The new dealer appeared, showed his hands, opened six new decks of cards and was placing them in the automatic shuffler. Diego was chatting with a player to his left. The cocktail waitress appeared to Diego's left with a fresh cup of coffee. Diego had already turned left to chat with his neighbor, so he nodded thanks to the cocktail waitress and simply reached his left hand out to get the coffee cup. Wait a minute! Dan reached over and paused the recording. He put it in slow motion reverse and backed it up to the point where Diego's left arm was outstretched, and his hand was opened up and about to grasp the coffee cup. Then Dan zoomed in on his hand. There… in between the thumb and first finger, in the fleshy fold of skin on the back of the man's hand, below and to the right of the knuckle of the first finger, were three dots, in the position of the points of a triangle. It was a small tattoo, and Dan recognized it. Just three little dots that, if connected, would form a perfect equilateral triangle. Dan knew that tattoo. Now he knew where he had seen that steely look before.

Chapter 9

As Dan walked back to his motel room that night, his brain was spinning. It had been more than 35 years since he had first seen that three-dot tattoo, long before he had joined the Crenshaw Detective Division in L.A. It had happened on his very first trip to Panama, on what was supposed to be a post-college journey of self-discovery. All the memories of that trip came back to him as he walked down the street in Reno that night, and he involuntarily shook his head and thought, "God, what a young, stupid, fucking idiot I was. I'm lucky I wasn't killed on that trip."

It was in the early '80s. The reason he had gone to Panama was to look for ayahuasca—or "yage" as it was called back then. He had read William Burroughs' book *The Yage Letters* while in college, and was fascinated by it. Dan was already fluent in Spanish from high school and college, and he started collecting obscure articles in Spanish on ayahuasca from South and Central America. Then a buddy of his, another yage enthusiast named Nate Alderson, told him that he had heard that there was this Peruvian *brujo* who had fled from Peru to Panama and was conducting traditional ayahuasca ceremonies up in the hills somewhere outside of Cerro Punta. Nate got this information from some other friend, who had heard it from someone else, and evidently that was good enough for the young Nate to talk Dan into flying with him to Panama City with their backpacks and tents, to catch a series of chicken buses up into the mountains in search of this witch doctor. Nate spoke no Spanish and needed Dan to interpret. When they eventually found this brujo, he talked with Dan for a few minutes and agreed to host Dan for a week-long ayahuasca ceremony for the equivalent of a hundred dollars. But he took one quick cold look at Nate and said to Dan in Spanish, "This one is not ready." When Dan asked why, the brujo only said that drinking ayahuasca was to be initiated into a process where there would be no turning back. But Nate would not be dissuaded, and pleaded with Dan to talk the brujo into hosting him as well. The brujo finally agreed when Nate offered him five hundred. The week-long "religious ceremony" basically consisted of the brujo letting the two young men repeatedly drink a homemade, highly potent, psychedelic poison, and hopefully not die.

Years later, Dan came to appreciate that one of the main ingredients in ayahuasca was Dimethyltryptamine, or DMT, and that was only one of a few psychotropic alkaloids that had been identified in the ayahuasca brew. He didn't know what other ingredients this particular brujo used in his ayahuasca preparation—the recipe varied from indigenous group to indigenous group—but Dan and Nate spent a day helping this brujo gather various vines, leaves and berries, and then pounding them into a pulp, and then boiling that mixture down to a brown liquid. The brujo insisted that Dan and Nate eat nothing during this day of preparation, so by the time they drank the mixture late that first night, they were already weak and disoriented. Dan knew that part of the initial effects of the ayahuasca potion was "the purging" but he was not prepared for the next twelve hours of intense vomiting and diarrhea. Even though he had had no food that day—only water—he truly believed that every bite of food he had ever eaten in his entire life came out of him that night, out of both ends. By the next afternoon, when they woke up, both he and Nate were delirious, lying on the dirt floor of the brujo's hut, their clothes soiled with vomit and shit, when the brujo made them drink the potion again.

It took Dan years to remember and connect all the different experiences he had that week—or rather, that his soul had experienced and he had witnessed that week. When he finally came to, a week later, he was a filthy stinking mess, lying in mud in a hut. He got up and stumbled outside. The brujo was gone. He found Nate in another hut, both legs broken from some kind of fall. Dan found some protein bars in his knapsack and shared them with Nate, and then Dan hiked down to the nearest village to arrange for medical help. Eventually, after an agonizing two-day wait, Nate was transported to a Panama City hospital. Nate was traumatized and delirious, claiming he had been flying when his wings caught fire and he had fallen to the earth, breaking his legs. The doctors were able to put pins in his legs, and to arrange for transportation back to the states.

Dan, however, did not return to the states immediately. He hiked back up to the huts in the mountains and waited for the brujo to return. Dan was angry, and wanted to confront him. When the brujo finally returned, Dan yelled at him, asking him why he had left them, especially why he had left Nate with his broken legs. The brujo just stared at Dan and, after a long pause, said coldly, "He was not worthy."

Maybe it was the lingering effects of the ayahuasca, or maybe it was the disorientation of being in a foreign country. But at that moment, when the brujo said "He was not worthy", all of Dan's anger left him. The fact was, he couldn't disagree with that statement. Nate should never have tried ayahuasca. Nate was a pampered white kid from a well-off family who never had to worry about money. Nate was a good-time party guy. Nate was not the type of person who should have his soul revealed to him, because that soul was soft and contaminated in the way that only a life of wealth and ease can do.

Dan's own experience with ayahuasca was different than Nate's. When Dan eventually got back to California months later, he visited Nate. Nate had been so traumatized by the experience that his parents had had him hospitalized for many months. Still, in Nate's more lucid moments, he and Dan compared notes. Nate had seen demons, devils, angels, and horrible vistas; Nate still believed he had been given wings and was flying but that his wings had melted and he had plummeted to the ground. Dan had experienced nothing like those visual images. His ayahuasca journey was quite different, a journey without words and without images. During his sessions he found a cold silent part of himself that felt comfortable, reliable. He probably wasn't worthy either, but he had survived, and had changed. The pieces were fragmented, but over the next few years, he managed to put them together and understand them.

Dan had stayed with the brujo and underwent five more ayahuasca sessions before returning to the states. Each time, the process took him deeper to a place without words, without images. All in all, he spent two months with that brujo, studying with him, listening to him, learning what he could. But after two months, he was homesick, out of money, and he felt he had seen enough. So he returned to the States. When he left, the brujo gave him a small gift and urged him to come back to Panama and drink ayahuasca again. And Dan did return to Panama many times after that, ultimately "retiring" there. But he never sought out the brujo again, and he never again did ayahuasca, or any other psychoactive drug.

But that was not what Dan was thinking about that evening as he walked back to his motel. Those personal transformations were far, far in his past. What he was remembering was his brujo's tattoo: those small three dots that formed the points of a triangle in the flesh of the left hand between the thumb and the first finger. His brujo had explained that this was the tattoo of *un elegido*—one whom ayahuasca has chosen. He explained that ayahuasca chooses its elegidos from its *devotos*—its devotees—and that to be a devoto meant that once you drank ayahuasca, you were the servant of ayahuasca for the rest of your life. Dan had asked him, "Un devoto o un esclavo?"—a devotee or a slave?—and the brujo just replied, "Es lo mismo. Si la ayahuasca te elige, eres un elegido." "It's the same thing. If ayahuasca chooses you, you are a chosen one."

The brujo explained to Dan that with continual use, ayahuasca was capable of giving its devotos certain powers. Each devoto might receive a different power, or none at all. But if ayahuasca gave them a specific power, that meant they were "chosen," hence the terminology of being a chosen one—an elegido.

Dan also remembered the brujo's eyes, that intense quick cold stare, with the pupils always slightly dilated from the ayahuasca. It was the same glance that Dan had seen Michel Diego do in the video. Now Dan knew how Michel Diego was able to read the cards in the shoe. He wasn't reading them—he was *seeing* them.

Dan got to his motel room and immediately poured himself a drink and lay down on the bed. He was going to skip the hot bath tonight. He didn't want to relax—he wanted to think. He knew his thoughts didn't make any logical sense—he knew he could never, ever, explain it to Abe. But Dan knew without a doubt that Michel Diego was simply seeing, or intuiting, or somehow sensing, the next card in the shoe. That's why he never busted. That's why his eyes were always dilated. He was using ayahuasca to read the cards. Dan shook his head as if to shake that crazy idea out of his brain, but he knew it was true. No matter how crazy it sounded—which is why he could never tell Abe—Michel Diego was simply looking at the next card in the shoe, seeing what it would be even though it was face down, and then choosing to hit or stand based on whether that card would bust his hand or not. Dan's logical detective brain had to admire the pure simplicity of the con: no evidence of cheating, no evidence of card counting, no real work... it was the perfect scam, absolutely pure and simple, totally foolproof and totally undetectable... but some other part of Dan's brain was offended. He thought this was a betrayal of centuries of the sanctity of indigenous rituals and ceremonies. Over the decades, ever since that journey that he and Nate had taken, Dan had come to believe that it had been wrong for him—a North American, a gringo—to delve into the secret sacraments of the ayahuasca culture. He appreciated that he had survived the experience, and that he had grown from it. But he had ultimately concluded that it had been wrong for him to try it.

The brujo had once told him, "Gringos are like leaf-cutter ants—they build great cities, by destroying all the vegetation around them." It was true, Dan had come to believe. Gringos spread throughout the world, colonizing, gringo-izing, gentrifying, and ultimately destroying not only the ecology of the land but worse, the ecology and culture of the peoples who had lived there for centuries. Even in Villa Rosario, Dan had seen the commercialization, corruption and change that just a small influx of gringos had done to the town. Gringos who moved there to find paradise demanded WiFi, and WiFi brought the western world and U.S. culture to this sleeping village, and the young people started shooting that U.S. culture into their veins, and the way of life that had first attracted Dan to Villa Rosario ten years ago was eroding and would be totally gone in another decade.

But Dan had always told himself that he had tried to make amends for intruding into Panama's culture. He had tried to settle quietly in Villa Rosario and had tried to blend in; tried not to act like the typical loud-mouth, entitled, rich gringo. He bought from the local traders; made friends; tried to be kind, et cetera. The fact that he spoke Spanish really helped, because most gringos refused to learn Spanish—a fact that Dan always considered the height of arrogance. And Dan felt he had been successful in his efforts, that he had become acculturated and was accepted by the locals. He even thought that helping don Fernando on a few slightly illegal projects was part of blending in to a culture that had a fair amount of corruption. In fact, he was proud of himself for making a successful transition, for being accepted. He thought he had "made it."

And maybe that's why the murder of that suspect in the jail cell came as such a shock to him. He thought he knew the culture, that after ten years of blending in, he had become "one of them." So when don Fernando simply explained to him after the killing, "That's what we do down here," it came as such a shock to him. He didn't know that, he didn't expect that, and worst of all, he couldn't accept that. Even in difficult cultures with different languages, rituals and customs, he thought there *had* to be common values. You just don't kill someone because they're a bad person. Even the worst person gets some kind of due process.

That was the gringo way.

Dan got up and poured himself another drink and then lay back down on the bed. He tried to push aside all his personal turmoil at that moment and focus on what he was going to do about Michel Diego. His job was to protect the casino from theft. Well, he thought, that coincided with his personal wishes. He was going to have to convince Michel Diego never to come to the casino again. Dan never wanted to see him again, never see that tattoo again, never wanted think about those memories again. He had enough problems trying to process the murder in La Chorrera without trying to dredge up drug-induced hallucinations from over three decades ago. Somehow, Dan had to bar Michel Diego from the casino. That would serve both purposes: protect the casino and allow Dan to lock those old memories back up in the vault where they belonged.

Dan took another sip of whiskey and thought about this. Yes, this was the only solution. He would have to have a private talk with Señor Michel Diego and "convince" him not to come back to Barkley's, threaten him if necessary. That simply was how it would be.

Dan placed his whiskey glass on the small table by the bed. He closed his eyes to think about this. In a few minutes he was asleep.

The dream was dark, as if everything was bathed

in a brown light. He was standing barefoot outside a hut, stirring an old steel pot full of bubbling ayahuasca. The liquid was boiling down to a chocolate-brown liquid. Dan used a piece of screen to remove the last few leaves from the bubbling mixture. Soon it would be ready to drink.

Dan looked up. Nate was flying in circles about 30 feet above him. He had sprouted huge dark wings that flapped erratically, spasmodically. "I can't control this!" Nate shouted. Dan looked at him. Dan knew he was going to crash. Dan looked over to a patch of hard land on the other side of the huts. Dan knew that Nate was going to crash there in that field. Dan went back to stirring the large pot of liquid. Just a few more minutes now, he thought, and it will be ready.

"I can't control this!" Nate shouted again. Dan ignored him. He simply didn't care what happened to Nate, or rather, there was no point in caring. Nate was going to crash on that hard field over there, and there was nothing Dan could do to stop that. Nate would break both his legs. Dan knew this. There was nothing to do with this cold knowledge but to keep stirring the pot. Dan looked over towards the woods. In another minute, the brujo would emerge carrying an armful of vines and leaves. Dan continued to stir the pot. The odor was thick and pungent and mixed with the smoke from the fire below the pot to burn Dan's eyes. The brujo emerged from the woods carrying an armful of vines and leaves and walked over to Dan. Dan heard a scream and a crash as Nate smashed into the ground. Neither the brujo nor Dan looked over to the field. They both had known that would happen. There was nothing they could have done to prevent it.

Chapter 10

The next morning, Dan walked into the surveillance control room totally focused and committed to personally barring Michel Diego from ever entering the casino again, by whatever means necessary. He told Robbie, "If that guy shows up again, let me know. Even if it's my day off, call me. And give his picture to the other security officers and tell them the same thing."

Dan had made up his mind. He was determined. The problem was... Michel Diego never showed back up. The week passed, and the next week, and the week after that, with no sign of him.

Finally Dan concluded that Michel Diego might be gone. The majority of people who get Players Club cards only visit casinos once or twice and never return. Dan began to relax. It may have been a scam, but the con man was gone, and better yet, the reminder of all those long-ago memories was gone, too.

As the weeks passed, Dan began actually enjoying life. He was starting to find his groove in Reno. He kept score for Ashley's team a second time, and even went to watch her team play a few times when the regular scorekeeper was there. They had gone out to dinner again once and had started chatting in the casino during breaks.

And tonight they were having another date, once again down at Terri's

"I like this place," Dan was saying. "It's always quiet. When I leave the casino at night, the thing I appreciate so much is quietude."

"Is that a word?" Ashley laughed. "Quietude?"

"Sure, it's a word," Dan said. "It means a state of being quiet, tranquil."

"Is loudatude the state of being noisy? Or how about Quaalude—is that the state of being quaa?"

Ashley deadpanned.

"Ha," Dan said. "Maybe that's a good name for it... so-and-so is zoned out, he's so quaa."

"I used to use those... all the time," Ashley said, not joking.

Dan looked at her, realized she was being serious, and asked, "How long ago was that?"

"When I lived in Vegas... with John."

"That guy who beat you?"

"Yeah. He got me started on them. He told me they weren't addictive."

"The fuck they're not," Dan replied.

"Yeah," Ashley said. "I know that now. When I moved here, my therapist helped me get off them... She got me seeing a real doctor, not that quack John got those pills from.... My therapist always used to say that there's only one addiction, but that it shows up in many ways."

"What did she mean by that?" Dan asked

"Well, she said that I was the addiction— that it was part of my personality—and that I could never get rid of it; that I would always be addicted to something. But she also said that I could control what I was addicted to; that I had to *direct* my addiction, and take responsibility for it... so... now I bowl. I get real compulsive about it. The first thing I do every morning are my bowling exercises."

"Really?"

"Yeah, there are all these muscles that have to be stretched in certain ways. I went to a weeklong bowling workshop last year and learned them. They really helped my game."

"Well, I've watched you move," Dan said, "and you are so smooth, so fluid." He smiled. "I really like watching you play."

Ashley looked at him, smiled and looked down. Dan thought she might even be blushing a bit.

Then she asked him, "What about you? Did you ever do drugs?"

"Yeah, sure, but it was a very long time ago."

"Which ones?"

Dan didn't want to get into a discussion about it. "Oh, just different ones. It really was a long time ago. Now, I just drink... you know, in moderation... sometimes heavy moderation."

She laughed and parodied him. "Heavy moderation. Ha! That's a good one." Then she switched to a fake German accent. "Zo you are tellingz uz, Mister Landes, zat you af no addictions uzzer zan ze alcoholz?"

Dan laughed and then said, "Well, I've got my ruts... you know, patterns I get hung up in. I get stuck thinking about something and I just can't let it go. Part of that is the occupational hazard of having been a cop, I guess. I'm always in my head, trying to think things through. Even when I was living in Panama and just hanging out every day, my brain was always working, always trying to figure something out, trying to understand something. That's partly why... well no... that's *mainly* why I drink. It's the only thing that pushes the numb button on my brain. Only when I hit that second drink—never drunk mind you—but as the old song goes, comfortably numb. Then my brain shuts off and I can actually relax."

"You don't leave your thinking at the job? When you leave work?" Ashley asked.

"No, actually, that's when it starts up the most, after I leave work. At work, I'm just thinking about work stuff, you know, watching the video screens, looking for cheats, trying to figure out weak points in our security systems. But when I leave work—I don't mean now, because I'm here with you—but when I leave work, or have a day off, you know, any time I'm alone, my brain kicks into overdrive... I don't mean it's necessarily a bad thing, but my thinking can get into a rut."

"Like how?"

"Well... going over the same thing over and over again... but we don't need to talk about this, Ashley. These are my problems, just my personal boring problems."

Ashley reached out and touched his hand. "No, tell me. I want to know."

"Well, it sounds so stupid..." he started to say.

Dan paused, and shook his head. The truth was, he knew it wasn't stupid. He knew it was extremely important to him. It was just personal. But he liked Ashley, and he trusted her, and she was touching his hand, and somehow that made it okay, so he launched into it.

"I told you I saw some things that disturbed me in Panama..."

"Yeah?"

"Well,... there was this bad guy, a real meth-head whack-job hundred-percent asshole down there, and he murdered some people. We don't know how many, because, well, the police work in the small towns down there is pretty primitive and there is no record keeping to speak of. And this guy lived in the slums, but from what we pieced together afterwards, he appeared to be a serial killer who never got caught because he killed homeless people, drifters, unknown people. But he slipped up and killed a kid who was the son of a well-off family, and they demanded justice and paid for an investigation. In the rural areas down there, the police just don't have many resources. So if someone commits a crime against you and you want an investigation, you have to pony up the money for it."

"Wow, how weird."

"Yeah, but that's how it is in many poor countries. So anyway, that's how I got roped into it. I was friends with the police chief of the neighboring town, and he got called into the investigation, so he dragged me into it. Anyway, long story short, we caught the guy, had him in jail, and we had some good evidence that we had sent off to the lab to be analyzed, and I was satisfied with the case. In fact I was very satisfied with it. I thought I had done a good job, that I had helped my friend don Fernando –"

"Who's he?" Ashley asked.

"Oh, he is police chief of the town where I live. He's the one who roped me into the case after he got called into it. And he is—or was—my best friend down there. We had been friends for almost ten years. Anyway, I thought I had really helped him out, and had helped the community out. And, I figured my job was done. We had the evidence. We had the suspect behind bars. I figured he would be arraigned in court, set for trial, convicted, and put in jail for the rest of his life or so. But I didn't know that there is this old, ancient, tradition in Panama... not so much in the big cities, but in the rural areas where they still practice the old ways... this tradition whereby the family of a murder victim is allowed to simply kill the murder suspect without any trial, simply by making a traditional request to the police chief. In this case, there were two police chiefs involved, don Fernando, the police chief of my town, and Jorge Manuel, the police chief of the town where this kid was murdered. Anyway, the kid's parents made the request, the two police chiefs granted it, and while this suspect was handcuffed in his jail cell, don Fernando handed his pistol to the parents, and the parents took turns shooting this suspect to death through the bars of the cell..."

"That's horrible."

"Yeah, and I was there."

"You saw this?!"

"Yeah, I was standing right beside don Fernando when he handed them his gun."

Ashley just stared at Dan with her mouth open, shaking her head, and holding his hand.

"And what happened?" she asked.

"That's the horrible part," Dan answered. "*Nothing* happened. It was bad enough that I had to witness a murder—I had never seen anything like that before—but the worst part was that nothing happened, because..." Dan paused. "Because it's part of their culture. It's normal. It's accepted. It's understood. The parents knew they were going to do it. Don Fernando and Jorge Manuel knew the parents were going to do it. The entire staff of that police station knew they were going to do it... and..." Dan shrugged his shoulders. "And it was no big deal to them that it happened. I was the only one who didn't know it was going to happen."

"You couldn't turn them in to... someone?"

Dan shook his head. "What they did was perfectly legal."

Ashley looked dumbfounded. "But that's not right!"

"That's what I thought, too... what I still think... what I still want to believe," Dan said. "But it wasn't wrong *to them*... and I guess I still can't get my head around that. It bothers me. That's why I had to leave Panama, come back to the States and try to figure it out. I mean, I can't explain why it bothers me so much except that... well, for example, I knew some crooked cops in L.A. who were friends of mine. I knew what they did was wrong, but I just figured it was their choice to be crooked, and that eventually there would be some sort of karma for them. But a lot of them never got caught. They just worked up until the day they retired, and had all that extra money. And even that never bothered me, because I always knew what was right and wrong for *me*—I could always keep my actions separate from them. But in Panama, it was *my actions* that helped catch that guy; it was *my actions* that helped put him in a jail cell... and so... I couldn't keep myself separate from the consequences... I had always thought I was exempt from the bad things around me, but this time I wasn't." Dan paused. "I just don't quite know how to explain it," he finally said.

Ashley was quiet, just holding Dan's hand, and nodding. She looked deep in thought.

"Sorry to lay that horrible story on you, Ashley. Like I said, it's just my problem."

"No, no. I'm glad you told me. It makes a lot of sense. Sometimes I see you in the casino and you're just standing there watching something, but it's like your brain is miles away."

"Hmmm," Dan said, "Yeah, that's probably right."

"Let me ask you this, Dan," Ashley said, "You keep saying you want to go back to Panama. Why?"

That question made Dan sad. "Well, I used to fit in there, or at least I thought I did... I felt I did. After I quit the police force in L.A., I just didn't feel like I belonged in the States anymore. I didn't feel like I fit in. I wanted to go somewhere and start over. And I love Panama. I had been going there on vacation every year since I graduated from college. It's a magical country, great weather, beautiful scenery, beautiful people... That was the Panama I loved, and I want to believe that *that* Panama can still exist for me, that I can go back and be happy again... that I could go back and fit in again, feel like I belong again."

"And what would it take for that to happen?" Ashley asked.

Dan thought for a moment. "Time," he said. "Time, and I think I somehow have to forgive don Fernando. I mean, I know that sounds trite, but I haven't forgiven him yet. I used to look up to him. He is the law down there, and I always wanted him to... to value the things I did... He was like an older brother to me. That's why I always referred to him with the title 'don', out of respect."

"Oh," Ashley said, "I thought that was his name."

"No, it's just a title of respect, like 'the honorable,' that kind of thing. But anyway, after this thing happened, I started to think he was evil, because he should have resisted that honor killing bullshit. But now... now, I don't know. I don't think he's evil."

"He didn't think it was wrong?"

"Oh no! Absolutely not," Dan said. "Not in the slightest. That was what fucked me up. Even the most corrupt cops I knew in L.A. *knew* that what they were doing was wrong and against the law. But don Fernando absolutely believed, and still believes, that this was the right thing to do."

"Maybe he just says that to you," Ashley offered. "Maybe he has his own doubts, too."

"Hmmm... yeah, maybe."

"Did he ever murder anyone else?"

"Don Fernando?"

"Yeah, did he ever, you know, let any other arrested person get killed?"

"No," Dan said. "I don't believe so. He told me later that he and Jorge Manuel would not have done this except for the victim's family making the traditional request in exactly the right way. He said that he and Jorge Manuel were honor-bound to let the family kill that guy."

Dan thought for a moment, then added, "I mean, he was the basically the town sheriff, so yeah occasionally, he would bend the rules to get something done... he wasn't always legal... I remember one time, a couple of crooks moved into town and he just told them they had to leave or he would beat them up. He's a big guy, but he has this bigger reputation, so no one ever called his bluff. The threat was always good enough. He'd been the police chief for so long, nobody fucked with him. He kept the town safe... he actually did a lot of good. So it's hard for me to maintain the belief that he is an evil guy."

"I didn't used to think that John was evil, you know, because after every fight he would apologize and promise never to lose his temper again."

"But he'd do it again, right?" asked Dan.

"Yeah."

"I think that's evil..."

"It's a complicated subject," Ashley said.

"That's the truth," Dan said. "How long were you with him?"

"Almost two years, then I left him after he got arrested the first time, but then I went back for almost six months, but then that last fight happened... Then I got really scared of him. So I left Vegas."

Dan lifted his beer bottle and said, "Well here's a toast to us two renegades. May be both find happiness."

Ashley smiled, lifted her bottle, clinked it against his, and said, "To us."

Chapter 11

That dinner with Ashley was a turning point for Dan. It wasn't just the fact that he could tell her about the murder—it was the fact that she seemed to care... that he trusted her enough... liked her enough... well, more than just liked her... it was that confusing mixture of liking someone more than a little but not knowing how much, believing they feel something too but not knowing what, not knowing where any of it would lead, but really liking being with that person. More than just enjoying Ashley's company, Dan felt excited to be with her... he felt alive, happy.

And of course, that also meant he felt nervous, scared, and a little stupid for feeling so good, because there was that more-than-slight age difference between them. Yes, she seemed wise beyond her years, but her years were still far, far, behind his. And because of that, Dan restrained himself. It's not that he thought it would have been wrong to try and seduce someone that much younger than him, but he felt it would be wrong to try and seduce *her*—it was almost as if he liked her too much to risk offending her. Besides, Dan figured that if Ashley wanted that type of relationship with him, she—like most women—would find a way to let him know. In the meantime, he was happy to have someone to go to dinner with regularly, happy to chat with her in the casino during the day, happy to go watch her bowl occasionally.

And as he spent more time with her and got to know her better, she began opening up more with him, sharing bits and pieces of her life. He learned about her parents in rural Indiana, how they were very religious and used to beat her and berate her for any act of independence. She ran away twice, but the police always brought her back. She finally moved away permanently when she turned eighteen, and got involved with a series of controlling men. She struggled to make a living working as a waitress, first in Indianapolis, then Chicago, then California and finally Vegas. Along the way, she managed to get her B.A. in social work. Her hope, she had told him, was to save enough money to eventually go back to school and get her Master's.

It made Dan sad to hear about the series of abusive relationships she had been through. He wanted to broach the subject of how people repeat the same behaviors over and over until the underlying issues are resolved, but he felt like it would be hypocritical for him to do so, given his own life. Besides, she seemed to have a good handle on it.

And so the weeks unfolded in a pleasant rhythm of work, hot baths and whiskey, dinners with Ashley, and occasional evenings watching her bowl in the loud bowling stadium in downtown Reno. Life was good.

Then one day Michel Diego showed back up.

It was a weekday afternoon, like any other weekday. Dan had just returned to the surveillance room from having lunch with Ashley at the buffet. He was just sitting down at his console when Robbie called over to him.

"Hey Dan, you remember that guy about two months ago who kept winning at blackjack—the one who played so poorly?"

"Yeah?"

"He's back."

"What!?" Dan jumped up and went over to Robbie's console. His heart was racing. There was Michel Diego sitting at first base at a blackjack table, making bets.

"He showed up about 20 minutes ago," Robbie said. "I figured you'd be back soon so I didn't call you. I've been watching him play—it's exactly like before. Plays crappy but wins... doesn't bust."

"Pull up the table camera," said Dan. "Let me see his eyes."

Robbie adjusted some dials and Michel Diego's face appeared on one of the monitors. Robbie zoomed in on his eyes. They were slightly dilated.

"Okay, I'll be back." Dan said and got up and left the room. He made his way downstairs and walked up to the blackjack table. The dealer had just finished a hand and was collecting the cards.

Dan tapped Michel Diego on the shoulder, and flashed his security badge and said, "Señor Diego, por favor, venga conmigo. Traiga sus fichas," telling Michel Diego politely, but firmly, to gather his chips and come with Dan.

Michel Diego looked at Dan's badge, then gave one quick cold look at Dan, then smiled, nodded his head, and said in English, "Of course señor, my pleasure."

He gathered his chips and walked with Dan to a small conference room off the first floor. Dan gestured to one of the chairs at the small table and Michel Diego sat down calmly, just looked at Dan and waited, smiling slightly, as if everything was normal.

Dan sat in the chair opposite of him, and began: "Señor Diego, my name is Dan Landes, and I work in the security division here at Barkley's. Our job here is to protect the casino, to keep the games fair, and to make sure the casino is safe." Dan paused, and leaned forward. "And I have a favor to ask you."

Michel Diego looked a little surprised, and said, "Sí señor? What is it?"

Dan continued, "Well normally, when we catch someone cheating, we simply have them arrested. Even if they're not cheating but just engaging what we call 'advantage play', like counting cards, we can legally bar them from the casino by issuing a no-trespassing order against them. And if they show up again, then we can have them arrested. If we really don't like them, we can ask the Nevada Gaming Commission to bar them from any casino in the state..."

"Señor Landes," protested Michel Diego, "I have not been cheating. I play a little blackjack from time to time. It relaxes me. I just happen to be lucky at it."

"Don Michel," Dan said, using the term of respect, "I know what you have been doing. You've been using ayahuasca to see the next card in the shoe—that's *how* you've been so lucky. You are able to gain a huge advantage over the casino and anyone else at the table. It *is* a form of cheating."

Michel Diego's eyelids narrowed. "Really?" he said, "And how do you know this?"

Dan extended his left hand forward on the table, opening the space between his thumb and first finger and turning it so Michel Diego could see the three-dot tattoo on Dan's hand. That was the gift that the brujo had given him some thirty-five years ago before he returned to the States. The brujo had tattooed the small "elegido" tattoo on Dan's left hand.

Michel Diego's eyes widened as he looked at Dan's tattoo. Then he looked at Dan and smiled.

"Brother," he exclaimed, his smile widening. "I am honored to meet you. I rarely meet an elegido in the states."

"I've *never* met one here... before today," Dan said.

"But tell me brother," Michel Diego said, "hypothetically speaking, how would you prove to the authorities that I was cheating?"

"I couldn't," admitted Dan. "And that's why I said I have a *favor* to ask you. My job is to protect this casino, nothing more. I have no duty to any of the other casinos in town. I am asking you, as a favor, to not come here again. I will not tell any of the other casinos in town about you; I will not circulate your photo or your name to them. I will not tell the police that you have ayahuasca in your possession. I will not hamper your 'relaxation' in any way. I only ask that you not come back to *this* casino."

"I don't win very much," Michel Diego said, "just

enough to pay my bills. I only come to town and play this gringo game when I need a little money."

"I understand that, señor. And I can appreciate that. But there are many casinos here in Reno, certainly enough casinos to pay your bills and provide you comfortable places to sit and play blackjack."

Michel Diego sat for a few minutes, nodding his head and pursing his lips slightly. He looked at Dan's face and then at Dan's left hand.

"Your offer is fair, brother," he finally said. "I accept. And in return, I invite you to visit me. I live outside of town, in a humble house, in the desert. It is very beautiful and private there. We can prepare the ayahuasca tea together and be blessed with its gifts."

Dan felt a bit awkward. His intuition was that Michel Diego was telling the truth—that he was a longtime user of ayahuasca who lived by himself out in the desert and only came into town to make a little money. Dan almost felt an affinity with him. He could almost see Michel Diego's little house in his mind's eye—a simple hut off a dirt road with chickens in the yard. He reminded Dan of many older men he had met in Panama—people who kept a simple lifestyle and didn't bother anyone. And Dan also felt that Michel Diego's invitation, albeit naïve, was sincere. Dan had absolutely no interest in going to Michel Diego's house of course, or of ever drinking ayahuasca again. But he understood that for Michel Diego to invite a gringo into his house was a big deal.

"Don Michel," Dan said, "I very much appreciate your offer, but the rules of my job prohibit me from accepting your kind request."

"What are rules to men like us?" Michel Diego said with a twinkle in his eye.

"True... but still, I need... to follow my own path," Dan said.

"I understand, Señor Landes," Michel Diego said, "but if you change your mind, I'm sure that ayahuasca will lead you to me. It would be good to have someone join me in the ceremony."

Dan nodded.

"And now, I have taken too much of your time," Michel Diego said, standing up. "I will cash in my chips and be off."

"Before you go, don Michel, may I ask you one question?"

Michel Diego sat back down. "Of course," he said.

"Why cards?" Dan asked. "Why, of all the gifts ayahuasca could have given you, why blackjack cards?"

"That was partly my own doing," Michel Diego explained. "It started off as a delicate divination— being able to see just a little into the future, to know when something was just about to happen. But then I discovered that I could shape the gift, that with practice, I could bend it to something else. Ayahuasca's gifts are flexible, you know… I always liked cards so I learned how to 'aim' the eyes just for a second, to *feel* the cards… I don't really see them, but I know what they are. Since I came to this country, it has been a very useful skill…. And what about you, Señor Landes? What did Ayahuasca give you?"

Dan paused. He didn't intend to say it, but the words came out anyway. "I used to think it was the ability to know good and evil. But lately, I feel like I've lost that gift."

"Ah señor, once ayahuasca gives a gift, it never goes away. But sometimes it is necessary to drink ayahuasca again to make the gift stronger, to take it to another level. Another reason you should come and perform the ceremony with me."

Dan nodded his head. "Gracias don Michel, I will remember your kindness." Dan stood up and opened the door for Michel Diego. Michel Diego smiled, nodded his head, stood up and walked out of the conference room. Dan watched him walk across the casino floor straight to the cashier's window where he cashed in his chips, put the bills in his wallet and turned to walk out the casino's front doors, waving goodbye to Dan as he left.

Dan waved back and then headed slowly upstairs to the surveillance room.

"There are worlds around us," Dan thought to himself as he walked, "that are so different from what we know; and people from those worlds are standing right beside us. People so different from us they could be from Mars or Pluto. And most of the time we just have no fucking clue…"

He got upstairs to the surveillance room and poured himself a cup of coffee from the coffee pot. Robbie was watching him.

"What happened?" Robbie asked.

"He won't be coming back," Dan said.

"Was he cheating? I mean, how was he doing it?"

Dan knew he could never explain it, and that if he implied that Michel Diego was cheating that it would just lead to more questions, so he just said, "Well, let's just say he was winning too much."

"How did you get him to leave?"

"I just asked him."

"You just asked him?" Robbie exclaimed.

"Yeah, well sometimes you catch more flies with honey, you know."

"But how was he doing it?"

"Not in any way we could ever prove, Robbie. I just told him I knew he was winning too much, and things just kind of worked out that he agreed not to come back."

"Do you want me to list him on the 'no-trespass' list?" Robbie asked.

"No need, he won't be back. I take him at his word."

"You trust him?" Robbie asked incredulously.

Dan paused a second, and then said, "Yeah… yeah, I do."

Chapter 12

Michel Diego was true to his word, and never stepped foot into Barkley's Casino again. Dan knew this would be the case and felt immediately better. His little casino world was once again orderly, insulated, and protected. By persuading Michel Diego to leave, Dan had successfully repaired the iron fence around the tar pit of those ayahuasca memories. He no longer had to be reminded that there were brujos in the world capable of doing physically impossible things. He no longer had to consider how a few alkaloid molecules could summon forth real demons or real angels. He no longer had to think about how close he himself had come to flying and then falling out of the sky, probably to break his own legs. Life was regular and reasonable once again. "Maybe that's all reason is," Dan thought to himself, "the ability to jam baffle into the nooks and crannies of our consciousness, so the madness of other worlds doesn't invade our little islands. Maybe we need to believe in laws, customs, and personal codes to reassure ourselves that we're safe." He was reminded of that old quote from Voltaire: "If God did not exist, it would be necessary to invent him." He wondered if Voltaire meant that man needed to invent and believe in some type of god in order to live with the actual chaos and madness that exists in the world.

He mulled this thought over, in various ways, for several days after his encounter with Michel Diego. It helped him feel more sympathetic towards don Fernando. The thought that don Fernando needed to believe that honor killing was necessary to preserve—not just community safety—but don Fernando's own stable worldview somehow made don Fernando appear less evil and more like any other man who needed a crutch. It didn't make what had happened any more acceptable to Dan, but it made don Fernando more understandable. After all, Dan realized that he himself needed his own belief that every suspect got a fair trial, so that he could tolerate all the police abuses that he knew were happening every day when he worked in the Crenshaw District. Illegal searches? Well, at least the suspect would have the opportunity in court to challenge that search, or challenge the drug tests, or challenge whatever it was. That was the whole idea, Dan had always believed, behind the state's burden of proof—not only to give the suspect a chance to offset the advantage the police had, but to give people a way to believe that the judicial system was reasonable, even when they didn't like the outcome of that system. It kept life orderly, and it made it possible for Dan and millions of other cops to go to work every day and continue to be a policeman. Yes, there were criminals and madmen and horrible unspeakable violence on the streets in Crenshaw; But as long as he believed in the viability of the judicial system, he could regard all those madmen as renegades, or as deviants, who would eventually be caught and held accountable. His faith in that system made it possible to survive in the violent streets. And Dan had to admit that the honor killing system that don Fernando operated in provided the same psychological stability to don Fernando's world. Dan didn't have to accept that system, but maybe he could build a fence around it and learn to coexist with it. And if he could do that, maybe he could go back to Panama.

But then there was the problem of what to do about Ashley.

He and Ashley were spending more time together, and sharing more and more of their deeper thoughts. They coordinated their work schedules so they could have days off together. They hiked the Oxbow trails; they inner-tubed down the Truckee River. They went to the Planetarium and Museum of Art, and explored the restaurants and antique shops of Reno. They had moved from being friends to being something more, and

Dan could feel himself starting to develop feelings for Ashley.

They each had a three-day weekend coming up in two weeks and had started discussing going to Lake Tahoe together for the weekend. The discussion so far had been general, along the lines of "wouldn't it be fun" and wondering what it would cost. Dan knew that such a trip would inevitably force certain questions: Should they get separate hotel rooms or share a room? If they shared a room, would they be sharing the bed? Most couples ease themselves into bed with each other by "innocently" arranging external events to force them towards intimacy, and this seemed to be heading in that same direction. Dan decided to let it take its course. There didn't seem to be any need to push the river—it was flowing in that direction all by itself. Dan felt nervous but good about this evolution. He felt ready to love again, to be in love. He felt lucky that he had come to Reno, lucky that he had met Ashley, lucky that things were progressing well despite the age difference.

But then came the day when Ashley failed to show up for work. Dan was making the rounds of the casino floor at about ten Wednesday morning and stopped at the main casino bar where Ashley worked to see if she wanted to get lunch that day. But Tim the bartender told him that she hadn't shown up that morning.

"Oh?" Dan said. "Did she call in sick?"

"No," Tim said, "we haven't heard a word from her. I've sent her a text message, but no response."

"Huh... maybe she overslept," Dan said.

"I dunno."

Dan furrowed his brow. "Has she ever not shown up before?"

"Nope," said Tim. "First time."

"Okay," Dan said. "I'll check back later."

Dan also sent her a text message: "Everything ok?"

But he got no response.

He stopped by the bar again at noon, but Tim just shook his head no.

Dan called her but just got her voice mail. He left one message, then called back an hour later and left another message. He sent her another text. He started to worry. He remembered chatting with her the day before about her schedule today, so he knew that she hadn't simply gotten confused about what her day off was. He debated whether he should go over to her apartment building and ring the buzzer. He had never been inside her apartment building before. Maybe he was overreacting. But as the afternoon wore on, he decided he didn't care if he was overreacting. He would leave work at 5:00 and go there. If there was no answer, he would call the police. They could get in touch with the apartment manager and check her apartment.

But at 4:45 he got a text from her.

"Sorry. Things have been crazy."

He immediately texted her back. "Everybody's worried. What's up?"

She didn't text back immediately.

He waited.

About ten minutes later, he got a cryptic text.

"John's here. I'll explain later."

Dan's heart sunk.

He walked downstairs to the bar and waved at Tim. Tim walked up and said, "Haven't heard from her."

"I did," Dan said.

"Really? Is everything alright?"

"I'm not sure." Dan said. "I just got a brief text saying something crazy had happened and she would fill me in later." Dan didn't mention John. Then Dan thought for a minute, and said, "Wait. Tomorrow's her day off, isn't it?"

Tim looked at the schedule on the wall. "Yup, she's off tomorrow. She's back Friday."

"Ok, well, maybe she'll tell us Friday. Thanks, Tim."

"No problem Dan."

Dan clocked out and walked home. He stopped by the liquor store. His walk was heavier and slower than usual. He felt as if he had been hit in the stomach and had had all the wind knocked out of him. But he also felt worried. This guy John had assaulted her twice before. Did she have a no-contact order still in effect with him? He tried to think over everything she had ever told him about John. He couldn't recall if she had a protective order in place after the second beating or not. Probably not in effect anyway, he figured, too much time had elapsed. He felt stupid for not having asked her that question, for not being a good cop and knowing that answer.

Still, he thought, she's a big girl. She took responsibility for herself and moved out of Vegas after the second beating. She probably had talked with a number of police at that time. She had to have signed affidavits and promised to testify against him if necessary. She had moved to Reno. She had gotten into therapy. She had grown. She was a big girl. She could take care of herself. Who was Dan to be rescuing her? Maybe John had come to apologize. Maybe he had gotten into AA or something, had come to make amends. Maybe Dan was getting worked up about nothing. Maybe it was a happenstance encounter. Maybe John had changed…

But the more he thought about it, the more scared and angry he became. If there was one rule he could count on, it was that people don't change. He hated that rule, but it always seemed to prove itself. By the time Dan got to his motel room, he was furious. He put the bottle on the counter and texted Ashley. He knew he might be jeopardizing his relationship with her, but he just didn't care.

"What the fuck is going on?!! I know this is none of my business but I am VERY concerned. Please contact me."

He lay down on the bed and waited. The bottle remained unopened on the counter.

He didn't want to play the rescuer. He didn't want to play the cop, but he had a bad feeling about this. How did John get here? How did he find her? Why did she miss work? Something was wrong.

A few minutes later his phone vibrated. He looked at the incoming text message.

"I'm sorry. John showed up this morning. He wants to get back together. I'm sorry. I'll explain later. I'm sorry."

Dan reread it several times. He shook his head and reread it again. It might as well have been Greek— it just made no sense.

But now at least he could drink. There was something about being let down, about not being chosen, that was very recognizable to Dan. He knew how this worked. He got up and poured a full glass of whiskey and lay back down on the bed. His motel room suddenly felt very small, deflated, but very familiar. The exhilaration that he had been feeling the past several weeks was simply gone, as if it had never happened. But this was the world he knew, solitary but stable; cold and wordless, but solid. He wasn't used to having a girlfriend, hadn't gotten used to thinking of himself as part of a couple, and now that problem was gone.

Still, there was a nagging doubt. Something still made no sense; still didn't feel right. Her notes were too cryptic. But there was nothing he could do. He had texted her. She had answered. Case closed. Loose ends, but case closed.

Dan knew his own brain well enough to know when he had to do a forced reset. He got up and went into the bathroom and started running the tub.

He lay back down on the bed while the tub was running. There was something about American women, he thought... they always seem to evoke this protector in him. He never had that same feeling with Panamanian women. He thought back to Magali, the last woman he had "dated" in Villa Rosario. There was no real dating in the U.S. sense. They had been lovers, and he liked

Magali. But he didn't love her. Still, he never had the sense that in any way he had to look out for her, advise her, protect her, take care of her, or rescue her. She was simply a woman that he liked hanging out with. But Ashley was different. Why he didn't know... but he had these feelings for her... well, he thought, he would have to start rephrasing that now... he *used to have* these feelings for her. She was slipping through his fingers. Maybe she had already slipped through his fingers. Maybe she had never been in his hands at all. Maybe she had always been stuck on John, stuck in that dysfunctional relationship, and Dan was just a convenient person to hang out with until John showed back up... No, he thought, that was too harsh. She had suffered too much, had tried to grow, had tried to change... Oh, his fucking brain... why didn't it ever turn off???

He got up, went into the bathroom, turned off the water, tested the temperature with his hand, went back into the other room to refill his glass, got undressed, then carefully stepped into the bath and eased himself down. He took another sip. Ah, sweet whiskey, as he had thought so many times before, that doth knit up the raveled sleeve of care...

Chapter 13

The next day, Thursday, was rough. Dan made his rounds like a robot, checking the gaming tables, monitoring the slots areas, walking though the poker rooms. He sat and drank coffee and pretended to be looking at the video monitors, but in reality, his eyes weren't even focused on them. He felt completely disconnected from anything he was looking at.

At one point, he realized he was just killing time until Friday, until he could see if Ashley showed up for work or not, until he could actually see her, talk with her, maybe find out what was going on. She had said "I'll explain later" but Dan knew through experience that this expression rarely meant that any explanation was forthcoming.

Still, on one hand, he was glad that Ashley had the day off. It gave him time to prepare. He had been through this before. If their relationship was truly over, it was over. He didn't need to know why. He didn't need any explanation. If it was over, it was simply over. He didn't want to "be friends" in the sense of doing the same things they had been doing: having dinner, taking hikes, watching her bowl. He knew now that he did those things because he was falling in love with her... Damn, there he went again, he thought... He kept reminding himself that he had to put those feelings in the past tense... better to think of it as "he did those things because he *had been* falling in love with her." Best to put it all in the past now. Fun while it lasted. History now. Time to move on.

Come Friday, Dan didn't want to go to work. He actually thought about calling in sick, but he knew he couldn't do that, so he went in, determined to be a gentleman about the whole thing. But he walked into the casino via a different entrance than he usually took, one that would let him get up to the surveillance room without having to walk past the main bar where Ashley worked. From there he was able to keep one of his four cameras on the main bar. And he saw her come in a few minutes late, talk to Tim, then go in back of the bar to start her job.

Dan kept his other three cameras on various parts of the casino floor, so it would look like he was working, but he was mainly focused on watching Ashley. She cleaned the tables, took customer orders, relayed those orders to Tim, and then brought the customers their drinks. The bar had its normal early morning crowd. Dan was always amazed how many people started their day off with a drink, and then eased their way through the morning with more drinks, then had a cocktail at lunch, and then maybe one more drink before delving into the afternoon happy hour that started at 2:00 p.m. The drinks differed depending on the time of day: bloody marys and mimosas in the morning, or maybe coffee with Baileys or brandy, switching over to beer or wine for the early lunch crowd, but mixed drinks for the later lunch crowd, and then hard liquor for the rest of the day.

But Dan also knew that there was a natural lull that occurred around 10:00 a.m., when early risers left the bar to head to the tables before the late risers wandered in for their first eye-opener. So he headed down to the bar at 10:00. He didn't want to talk with Ashley, but he had to talk with her.

She was wiping down a table when he walked up behind her. "Hey," he said. She turned around. She looked like hell—the normal rosy tint on her checks was gone, and there were slight dark circles under her eyes.

"Oh, Dan... hi," she said, but her eyes were darting around, as if she was afraid to look him straight in the face. "Um, look, I guess I owe you an explanation."

"No," Dan said, "You don't owe me anything, but I need to know if you're okay."

"Yeah, yeah, I'm fine... John showed up... well I guess you know that... we talked all night... I don't... well... he wants to get back together. The state sent him to rehab and to anger management, and I can tell he's different. I feel like I owe him a chance."

Dan bristled. "You don't owe him anything, Ashley."

"Yeah, you're probably right, but I'm going to see if he's really changed. I'm going to make him prove himself. My eyes are open this time, Dan... but I want to see if it can work."

Dan shook his head left and right imperceptibly, and then asked, "Where's he going to stay?"

"With me," Ashley said, and realized how that sounded, and quickly added, "I mean, he just got to town and didn't have a place, so he asked if he could crash on my couch, and I told him okay."

Dan's headshaking was now perceptible. He pursed his lips. He didn't want to say what was in his head—he knew he would be overstepping his relationship with her—but he said it anyway.

"Look, Ashley, if he had really changed, he would have made arrangements in advance for a place to stay. He would have respected your boundaries and not just shown up 'with no place to stay'. It's not like there are no motels in Reno, you know."

He could feel Ashley stiffen up.

"It's my choice, Dan," she said flatly.

"Okay, okay, I'll back off," he said. "I think this is a mistake, but you're right, it's none of my business." He started to turn and walk away, and then added, "Just be careful."

"I will," he heard her say over his shoulder.

*   *   *

And that's how it was for the next three weeks. Dan no longer looked at Ashley's bar on the video monitors up in the surveillance room; he started leaving his shift ten minutes after it ended so he wouldn't run into her leaving her shift; if they did pass each other on the floor in the casino, they would each nod their heads to acknowledge the other person, maybe say "hey", but there was no conversation; there were no more dinners; no more hikes; no more scorekeeping; no more bowling nights.

But Dan had been around; he knew how this thing worked; the trick to structuring time is keeping a solid routine—a rigid routine—in place, never allowing any unstructured free time to come in before one is ready. And so Dan simply got up every day, walked to work, did his job, walked home, stopping at the liquor store on the way home. He made checklists on 3x5 cards, listing everything he had to do that day. Once each task was done, he would cross it off the list. He structured time the same way that many prisoners that he used to know would structure their time—slowly, methodically, hour by hour, day by day. And that way the hours went by, pulling the days along with them.

And as the days went by, Dan turned his focus to the idea of going back to Panama. He began writing down thoughts of what it would take for him to feel comfortable enough to return. He made lists of the steps he would need to take in order to go back. He would have to sell his car, give notice at Barkley's, and purchase airline tickets. He realized he would have to sell the gun that he had purchased in Vegas when he got his armed security guard license. He couldn't take that back to Panama, and he didn't want to. He had only gotten the armed security guard license as opposed to the regular security guard license because it opened up higher paying jobs to him, and then of course he had to get a gun to go with the license. No point in having an armed security guard license without an arm to go with it, he had told himself at the time. But truth be known, Dan did not like guns. He had been issued one when he worked in the Crenshaw District, but he kept it locked in the safe at work and never wore it. He simply didn't need it as part of his white-collar crime investigative work. He knew how to shoot, of course. His training had been good, and he had a steady hand. But he just never developed the fetish for guns that so many of his colleagues had. And of course, after the murder in La Chorrera, when he witnessed how the firepower from don Fernando's gun put a hole in that suspect's chest and then blew off the side of his head, Dan never wanted to touch a gun again. But he knew that prospective casino employers would expect him to have a gun, and so he had purchased a used Ruger LC9 in Vegas, the smallest lightest sidearm that he could find. As an armed security guard, Barkley's expected him to carry his gun, and so he did, in a shoulder holster under his left arm.

Finally the day came when Dan sent an email to don Fernando—a long rambling email—saying that his time away from Panama had been good for clearing his head; apologizing for the many arguments he had started with don Fernando after the shooting; saying he was thinking of coming back to Panama soon; and expressing the hope that they could still be friends.

Don Fernando wrote back right away, saying that he always considered Dan to be part of his family, and expressing the hope that Dan would return to Villa Rosario soon. Don Fernando referred to Dan as "Dani" in his email, a nickname that don Fernando always used with Dan, and it made Dan smile when he saw that.

But that all changed in the middle of the fourth week.

It was a Wednesday morning. Dan had left his motel room and was walking to the casino. Dan liked the early morning walk. The air was cool. It was too early for the sun to turn the streets into the broiler pans they would be by noon. The trash trucks were making their rounds. A few homeless men were sleeping in various doorways. Dan was enjoying the walk when his cell phone vibrated. He pulled it out of his pocket and looked at it. It was a text from Tim asking him to stop by the bar when he got to work. Dan wondered what the problem was. If there had been an early morning drunk or some monetary loss, Tim should be calling the security guards on duty, not him. He began to get a bad feeling in his stomach and quickened his pace to the casino.

When he got to the main bar, Tim was waiting for him.

"Ashley's up in the coffee shop by the buffet," he said. "She needs to talk to you."

Dan's eyes narrowed, and Tim added, "She's pretty messed up."

Dan walked briskly up to the coffee shop. Ashley was sitting at a side table. She looked up as he sat down. Her eyes were puffy and there was a red swelling on her left cheek.

"Dan... I fucked up," she said.

He could see tears welling up in her eyes.

"John?" Dan said.

Ashley just nodded as tears started to roll down her cheeks.

"He's drinking again?" Dan asked.

Her lips were quivering. She could only nod her head yes.

"Still living with you?"

She continued to nod yes and cry.

"And he hasn't found a job?"

She shook her head no.

"And you're fighting all the time?"

She nodded her head yes.

"And last night it got bad, and he hit you," Dan said.

Tears were pouring out of her eyes now as she nodded yes. She pulled a wad of paper napkins from the dispenser on the table and blotted her face with them.

"I'm sorry to sound like a cop, Ashley, but it's just such a classic situation."

She continued nodding and crying.

"Look Ashley, I'm no social worker. You need a counselor to talk with. I'm just an old ex-cop, so I can only ask you one question—what are you going to do?"

"I don't know Dan," she sobbed. "I told him to leave a couple of times, but he says he has no place to go."

"That's not exactly your problem, Ashley. But... ah... what I was *referring to* was the fact that he *hit* you. This would be his third domestic violence incident, right? Did you call the police?"

"I tried to, but he took my cell phone and threw it against the wall and broke it."

"Really?"

Dan tried to calculate how much additional prison time the felony of interfering with a 911 call would add to the felony domestic violence charge.

"I got scared, Dan. He was really drunk. He said if I ever called the police he would kill me. I promised him I wouldn't. I pretended to go to sleep. This morning I got up and pretended that everything was alright and told him I was going to work and I would see him tonight."

Dan nodded his head, and then said, "Look Ashley, this is a no-brainer. You need to call the police."

"I'm scared to, Dan."

"I know that. That's *why* you need to call the police. If you don't call them, the situation will only get worse. He's broken the law, Ashley. He's assaulted you. Not once, not twice, but three times. He's threatened you. He has to be stopped. That's what the police do. That's what the law does. It protects you from assholes like him...."

Dan paused and looked at her. "Look, Ashley, the way the system works is that once the cops get involved, everything is out of your hands. You know this. They take your statement; they investigate; they decide what the charges are; they arrest him; a prosecutor will talk to you, but the prosecutor decides how to prosecute the case. He'll get a fair shake but the process will all be out of your hands. That's how the system works; that's how it's supposed to work. But, in my opinion, *you* have to make the decision to get the police involved. If this had happened five or ten years ago, and I had learned what had happened... if you had been some neighbor and I had found out that you got hit, I would have made that decision for you. I would have called the police on my own, regardless of what you wanted. But I don't do that anymore. I don't want to be responsible for people's lives anymore. I won't make that decision for you. I think the police should be called. I think John needs to be held accountable. I will make the call for you if you want, but you have to ask me to."

"I don't want to send him back to jail."

"*You're* not sending him back to jail. If he ends up back in jail, it'll be because *he sent himself* back to jail. He's the one making all these bad choices. How many other women has he abused? How many other women will he continue to abuse if he's not stopped? ... Do you want me call the police or not?"

Ashley started to tear up again, but nodded her head yes.

"Will you come with me to the police station?"

"Of course. Anyone else know about this?"

"Tim knows a little. Marcie, the co-captain on the bowling team, knows everything. I've been texting her about it for weeks."

"Really?" Dan took out one of the 3x5 cards he carried in this shirt pocket. "What's her full name and phone number?"

Ashley gave it to him and he wrote it down.

"Okay, Ashley, just sit right here." Then as he stood up, he asked, "Do you want a cup of tea?"

"Please."

Dan went over to the counter and asked the waitress to take Ashley a cup of tea. He then sat down about eight tables away from her, out of earshot range, and got out his cell phone. First he called Robbie up in the surveillance room.

"Hey Robbie, it's Dan. I'm down on the second

floor with a domestic violence case. Can you call that lady cop friend of yours, the blond lady that works domestic, whatshername? Yeah, Susan, that one, can you call her and find out if she's working and if so, tell her I'm bringing a victim in to talk with her, and maybe a witness too, and tell her that the perpetrator has already got two prior convictions for domestic assault, and also that he forcibly kept this victim from calling 911 last night? Yeah. Call me back when you get a hold of Susan and let me know where to take this girl and what time. Thanks."

Then he called Marcie and introduced himself, told her what was going on, and explained that her cell phone contained evidence, specifically the texts that Ashley had been sending to her over the past several weeks. He asked if she would be available that morning to meet him down at the police station. She told him she would be glad to help, that she had been trying to talk Ashley into getting out of that relationship for weeks. He told her he would call her back as soon as he had the exact location of Susan's office and the time to meet down at the police station.

Robbie called Dan back as soon as Dan got off the phone with Marcie. Susan could see him now. Robbie gave him the address. Dan called Marcie back and relayed the information.

Dan went back to where Ashley was sitting with her tea and said, "Ok, we've got an appointment downtown. Are you ready?"

A look of dread crossed Ashley's face.

Dan gave her a smile and said, "You can do this. Come on, we'll let Tim know what's going on first. Come on."

Ashley stood up. Dan took a few steps toward the cashier and reached for his wallet, but the cashier just waved her hand "no" to him. On the house. He nodded thanks and took Ashley by the arm and walked her downstairs. They stopped by the main bar and Dan told Tim he was taking her down to fill out a police report and she'd be back later to work the afternoon shift. Tim nodded.

Down at the police station, Marcie and another bowling friend, Mary Ellen, were waiting for them. Dan was glad that Ashley had emotional support. Susan talked briefly with Dan first, and he gave her the overall picture and his business card. Then Susan wanted to talk with Ashley. This, Dan knew, would take several hours. Dan told Ashley that he had to get back to the casino but that when she was done, to call him, and he would come down and walk her back to work. Marcie and Mary Ellen volunteered to wait, to take Ashley to lunch after the interview, and said that they would then make sure she got back to the casino. Dan thanked him and explained that it was important that Ashley come back to the casino to work that afternoon. He didn't tell them, but he assumed that if all went smoothly, that John would be arrested that afternoon, and Dan wanted Ashley safely at work that afternoon.

As Dan walked back to the casino, he thought about what it felt like to be back inside a U.S. police station again. He had noticed it the moment he had stepped inside the station with Ashley—the "feel" of the place. In the same way that hospitals all have a certain smell, he mused, police stations all have a certain feel. It's a feeling of being on edge, alert, on guard. It's the vibration of fear from witnesses and victims, and the counter vibration of calm and controlled moral outrage from the police. He was glad he no longer had to work in that environment, but at the same time he was grateful that the police system was in place. There was no such system in Panama, at least not in the small towns. If a boyfriend beat up his girlfriend, this was a family matter, and not something the police would get involved in. However, if the girl's father or brothers beat up the boyfriend in retaliation, that was also a family matter and not something the police would get involved in, either. He knew there was a certain balance of power in the Panamanian system. No guy wanted to go against his girlfriend's entire family. But all in all, Dan preferred the U.S. system. It eliminated that "Hatfield-McCoy" phenomenon in Panama where the family of the boyfriend would then beat up the brothers of the girlfriend in retaliation for the boyfriend getting beat up. When the U.S. police and court system got involved, people backed off and let the system take its course.

Dan was thinking these things as he walked along, thinking he had done the right thing today, thinking that Ashley was in good hands with the Reno domestic violence department. It was the right thing to do. The world felt rational. Then he turned the corner and saw Michel Diego standing at the entrance to Barkley's, waving at him.

Chapter 14

Michel Diego was gesturing to Dan to come over and talk with him. Dan walked up and said, "Sí señor?"

Michel Diego gave Dan a quick sharp cold look, as if he was looking through him. Dan could see his eyes were slightly dilated.

"Ayahuasca came to me last night," Michel Diego said.

"Yeah?"

"And told me that you would need to partake soon," Michel Diego continued. "Ayahuasca says you need to drink. I did not want to wait for you inside..." He gestured back towards the casino entrance. "Because I gave my word. But I brought you a gift."

Michel Diego undid the button of his jacket and held the left side of the jacket open slightly. There was a large pocket inside the coat, and in the pocket was a clear plastic soda bottle filled with a dirty dark brown liquid. Dan felt his neck and back stiffen up. He recognized that liquid. But after the morning he had already had, Dan was not feeling very patient, certainly not feeling like humoring a whacked-out old juice head.

"Look, I'm not in the mood for this, señor," Dan said. "I already told you I don't want to drink. Now please, close your jacket and go home."

Michel Diego closed and buttoned his jacket, smiled and said, "I told ayahuasca you would not accept my gift, but that I would give you this instead."

He reached into his pocket and pulled out a piece of paper and handed it to Dan. Dan took it and looked at it. It was an address.

"I am home most of the time. I will have some of the potion waiting for you when you come."

"I'm not coming," Dan said forcefully.

"Ayahuasca says you need her and you will come."

"And why would I need her?" Dan asked.

"Because you need her gift."

"I have to go to work now, Señor Diego," Dan said. "Please go away."

Michel Diego nodded as if to accept Dan's command. Dan started to step around him and into the casino. "Don't lose my address," Michel Diego said as he turned and walked away.

Dan thought to himself, "I won't. I'll keep it in case I ever have to have you arrested. Jesus fucking Christ, what else can go wrong this morning?"

He walked over to the main bar and gave Tim an update.

"Thanks," Tim said. "I don't want to lose her. She's a good worker."

Then Dan went up to the surveillance room and filled Robbie in.

"Jesus, man," Robbie said. "I had no idea. That's fucking nuts. Ashley's a good kid. I hope they put that guy away."

But as it turned out, they didn't put him away.

Marcie and Mary Ellen brought Ashley back to the casino after lunch and she seemed better. But when the police went to her apartment later that afternoon to arrest John, he was gone, along with all his things. Susan came by the casino to pick up Ashley to make sure that John had not stolen anything from her apartment.

Susan called Dan to relay the news.

"The warrant's in the system," she told Dan. "It's just a matter of time before we pick him up. Ashley described his car to us—it's an old silver Toyota Corolla sedan. We got the license number from the DMV. We'll find him."

"He must have known he went too far last night," Ashley said to Dan. "All his clothes and stuff are gone. He must have gone back to Vegas. I don't think he'll be back."

Dan wasn't so sure. He arranged for a locksmith to change the lock on Ashley's apartment door. Ashley called her apartment manager and explained the situation. Dan suggested that Ashley get a room in the casino that night. Ashley said no, but she did ask Marcie to stay with her that night. Dan also went down to the mall with Ashley and she got a new cell phone. She put Dan's number on speed dial.

When Ashley's shift ended late that afternoon, Marcie and several of her teammates showed up at the casino to take Ashley to dinner. Dan went down to the bar to talk with Ashley before she left with them.

"What time do you think you'll be done with dinner?" he asked.

"Well, probably 8:30 or so. I have to work tomorrow so I can't stay out late."

"Okay," Dan said. "Do me a favor. When you and Marcie get back to your apartment, will you text me that you're safely back there?"

"I will," Ashley said.

"Don't forget."

"I won't."

"And if there is any sign of him, any sign at all," Dan said, "call 911. Don't try and talk with him; don't try to assess the situation; don't even think; just dial 911. Promise?"

"I promise." She gave Dan a hug. "Thanks Dan, I really appreciate all you've done for me. I'll be fine tonight. Marcie will be with me. Let's do lunch tomorrow."

"Ok," Dan said. "Don't forget to text me tonight."

"I promise," she said.

But Dan still felt uneasy.

As he walked back to the motel that evening, he kept turning it over in his mind. Why would John just pick up and go? Did he know that Ashley had gone to the police? Or was Ashley right, that he had realized that he had gone too far and wanted to get out of town before Ashley decided she had had enough? Or did he have some other woman on the side, a new potential victim he had met during all those days when Ashley was at work? Or had some other thug shown up to settle some totally unrelated score? Dan just didn't know. Ashley's explanation seemed the most obvious, the most rational, the most logical.

Dan stopped by the small market and bought a few groceries for dinner. He skipped the liquor store because he still had some whiskey left at the motel, and besides, he wasn't really feeling like drinking much tonight. He felt worn out.

That night after a hot bath and after dinner he still felt unusually tired. He lay down in bed, thinking he would just rest a bit, but he quickly fell asleep. Maybe it was all the stress of the day, or worrying about Ashley, or maybe it was the hope that his relationship with her might be rekindled, but whatever the reason, he fell into a deep, deep sleep.

He was back in the jungle, stirring the large cauldron of ayahuasca leaves. Nate was flying in erratic circles above him. Dan looked over to the grove of trees. He knew the brujo would emerge from the trees in a few minutes with more vines and leaves. Dan looked down to the bubbling brown mixture. The smoke from the wood fire was combining with the ayahuasca smell to make that thick pungent smoky odor. The scent of it seemed to infuse his body, infiltrating his pores and flooding his blood cells. He looked over to the grove of trees. The brujo was emerging with an armful of cut vines and leaves. But there was someone walking beside him. Dan squinted to see. It was Ashley—she was walking beside the brujo, her head hanging down, her hair in her face. Dan dropped the large wooden paddle he had been using to stir the ayahuasca. He wanted to move, but his feet seemed stuck to the ground. He could only watch as the brujo and Ashley walked slowly towards him. As they got closer Dan could see smears of blood across the top of Ashley's blouse. Her arms were behind her back, and Dan knew they were tied at the wrists. The wind shifted, and the smell of bubbling ayahuasca blew into his face. He took a long deep breath of it and let it fill his lungs. He gave Ashley a quick hard cold glance, and knew something was horribly wrong.

Dan woke up in a panic. He looked at his watch. It was past 11:00 p.m. He grabbed his cell phone. Ashley had not texted him. He called her number. It rang five times and then went to voicemail. He found the card with Marcie's phone number and dialed it. Also no answer. He hung up and dialed 911 and quickly explained the situation. He knew that he didn't have much to tell them, so he made sure to tell the police operator that he was a retired L.A. detective, and told her to call Susan at home to verify everything he was saying. A desk sergeant got on the line and Dan told him the same thing. The desk sergeant took him seriously and said he would send a unit over to the Balboa Apartments. Dan said he would meet them at there.

Dan put on his shoes, then his shoulder holster and gun, and then his jacket over his holster. Then he went outside and got into his car and drove to Ashley's apartment. On the way there, he dialed Ashley's number again. Still no answer.

A police cruiser was waiting when he showed up. Two young cops explained that they were waiting for the apartment manager to show up with a key. They had tried the doorbell downstairs to Ashley's apartment but there was no response.

The apartment manager showed up a few minutes later, grumbling about having to come out this late. He opened the front door and the two officers went in with him. Dan started to go in, but they gestured for him to wait outside.

The few minutes that Dan stood there in front of

the apartment building seemed like an eternity. He tried to tell himself that everything was going to be alright—that he was just overreacting. He took in a deep breath of air to try and relax himself. The smell of pungent ayahuasca filled his lungs. He jumped, looked around, and quickly blew the breath out of his lungs. He sniffed the air. There was no ayahuasca smell. "I am starting to lose my fucking mind," he thought to himself.

Just then one of the young cops came running down the stairs and out the front door, running straight to the police car. Dan wanted to move but his feet felt stuck. The apartment manager stumbled out, looked pale and shocked, leaning against the building wall for support. Dan could hear the cop calling for an ambulance. He inhaled, smelled a wisp of ayahuasca again, and suddenly his feet were free, and he ran into the building and up the stairs.

Ashley's door had been jimmied open. Through the open door he could see the other cop kneeling down over a body. Fear filled him. He stepped inside and looked over the officer's shoulder. It was Marcie. Her head was bleeding badly. Dan ran into every room in the apartment, looking for Ashley but she was not there. He went back into the front room. The first cop had come back upstairs with a first aid kit and was applying a compress to Marcie's head to stop the bleeding. It looked to Dan that she had been hit across the side of her head with something hard. But she was alive. Unconscious, but alive.

The first cop looked up and said to Dan, "You need to wait outside, sir. The ambulance will be here in a minute."

Dan nodded and went downstairs. He knew the protocol. Preserve the crime scene as much as possible. He had instinctively known not to touch anything as he had run into each room. His cop brain was kicking in. He got to the downstairs outside door to the building and looked at the lock. It had not been tampered with.

John must have made a duplicate key to that door. However, Ashley's apartment door had those classic burglary crowbar marks. Dan had instantly recognized the splintered wood pattern left by those specially altered crowbars that burglars use. So John must have anticipated that she would change the locks and brought a crowbar.

Dan was watching the whole scene in his mind's eye. John used his key to enter the front door. He went up to Ashley's apartment. He didn't knock or do anything to announce his presence. Why? Because, Dan realized, he knew that Ashley had gone to the police. He knew she had changed the lock to her apartment door. If Marcie or Ashley had heard him trying to use his old key, they would have called 911. He had jimmied open the door with one snap of that special crowbar, and then immediately struck Marcie across the head with it, knocking her out. But why no screams? Did it all happen that fast? Or were the neighbors not home?

Another squad car pulled up. Susan and another woman police officer got out. Susan was dressed in civilian clothes. She nodded at Dan and ran upstairs. The other officer came over to Dan and she started asking him questions. An ambulance pulled up, and two ambulance attendants carried a stretcher and supplies upstairs. A third ambulance attendant was talking to the apartment manager, making sure he was okay.

Dan was talking to the other female officer but his mind was racing. Marcie didn't scream because John had hit her so fast. He could see Ashley running into the front room from the kitchen. Why didn't she scream? Because John had a gun. Dan could see it. He has a gun. Shit.

"I need to sit down," he said to the officer.

"Of course sir, we can take your statement later."

Dan sat against a small retaining wall. He didn't know how he knew that John had a gun, but he knew. He could somehow see it.

Susan came downstairs and went up to Dan.

"Mr. Landes, I am so sorry. We've notified every patrol car in the city to search for that silver Toyota."

"He's taken her somewhere," Dan said. "I can sense it."

"Do you have any idea where?" Susan asked.

Dan just shook his head. "No." The he added, "I should have made her stay in a hotel tonight."

"You had no way to foresee this," Susan said.

"I should have," said Dan and stood up. "I should have foreseen it."

"Go home, Mr. Landes. I'll call you as soon as we know anything."

Dan looked at Susan. He couldn't tell her what he was going to do, so he just said, "I'm going to just drive around. An extra set of eyes can't hurt."

"Mr. Landes..." Susan looked concerned. "I know you're a retired police officer, but let us handle this. We'll find him."

"I'm just going to look. I'll call if I spot his car."

She still looked concerned, but said, "Okay."

He turned and walked to his car. When he got inside, he reached into his jacket pocket and fished out Michel Diego's address. He typed the address into his cell phone's GPS. The address was at least ten miles outside of town, south of Lockwood, Nevada. Dan started his car and headed towards Interstate 80.

Dan knew that the police would not find John. He had seen that in the vision of John walking up to Ashley's apartment door with that crowbar in his hand. John had somehow found out that Ashley had gone to the cops. Maybe he had followed her to the casino and then followed her and Dan down to the police station. But in that vision of John and the crowbar, Dan could see John's determination, that total fanatical determination that only an insane sociopath is capable of. Ashley was the focus of all his hatred and rage for everything that had gone wrong in his life. He was not going back to jail. And if he did, she would pay. And by now, Dan calculated, John had had enough lead time to get out of Reno with Ashley. The police would not find him within the Reno city limits. But where was he? Which direction had he taken?

It took Dan twenty-five minutes to get to Michel Diego's little house. It was at the end of a dirt road. There was no number on the house, but the GPS said this was it. Dan got out of his car, walked up to the front door, and knocked.

After an interminable wait, the door opened. There was Michel Diego, looking a bit disheveled, but smiling.

"Ah, Señor Landes, yes, please, come in."

Dan stepped inside. The tiny cabin was in complete disarray.

"Tell me Michel, how you see the cards," Dan barked.

"I just give them a quick look and I can tell. I don't see them, but I know. It's like they speak to me."

"No, no, no, I mean, how do you use ayahuasca to see the cards?" Dan said.

"Oh, yes, of course, the trick is... well for me, it's different now. I've used it for so long. I just need one small cup a day... but when I was starting out with the cards, it was little sips. The ceremonies are one thing, you know, to feel the full power, the full majesty of it, to be swept away, to receive the gifts, to be chosen... but to *manage* the gifts, that's different. Little sips, one every five minutes or so. When I was first starting out I would bring a flask to the table. Everyone thought I was an alcoholic... I don't need that now, but you should do that."

"I need to find someone..." Dan started to say.

"Yes, yes, I know," Michel Diego interrupted him. "Wait here."

Michel Diego went into the other room and returned with a plastic soda bottle filled with brown liquid.

"One big sip now," Michel Diego said pointing

to a chair. "Sit down and take one big sip, and let me watch you. If ayahuasca agrees to take you, then you can leave, and just continue to take small sips every five minutes until the bottle is gone."

He handed the bottle to Dan. Dan took it, unscrewed the top and put it to his lips. That smoky pungent odor hit his nose. The taste—that sweet strong sour taste—hit his mouth. He swallowed, screwed the top back on the bottle, sat down, and waited.

Nothing was happening. He looked at Michel Diego. Michel Diego was looking at him, just smiling. Dan looked at the backs of his hands. They seemed normal. Then his felt this warm glow from his stomach. He hoped he wouldn't be sick.

"You won't be sick," he heard Michel Diego say, as if he was reading Dan's thoughts, "not with small sips." But then Dan realized that Michel Diego's mouth hadn't moved. Dan wanted to say something but he felt his thoughts turning to liquid and flowing through his hands.

"Get up!" he heard Michel Diego say loudly. Dan realized he was lying on the floor, and Michel Diego was shaking him. How did he get to the floor? He hoisted himself back to the chair. His stomach felt a little queasy but otherwise he felt normal. He looked at the backs of his hands. They seemed normal. He looked at his watch. Thirty minutes had somehow passed from when he had gotten to the house. Where did the time go? Where did he go?

"You're as ready as you're going to be," Michel Diego said. "Take a small sip and tell me why you need this power."

Dan looked around. The plastic bottle was on the table by the side of his chair. He screwed the top and took a small sip, replaced the top and slid the bottle into his jacket pocket.

"This guy has taken this girl," Dan said. "Kidnapped her. I need to find them. I think he's left town with her but I don't know where they went."

"Do you know this guy?" Michel Diego said.

"No."

"Do you know this girl?"

"Yes."

"You must concentrate on her. Keep her image, her essence, in your mind but only look at it in short quick bursts. Don't let your eyes linger on her image. Ask ayahuasca to lead you to her. Get into your car and just drive. Take little sips and make quick little glances at her. Keep asking ayahuasca for guidance. Go now." Michel Diego gestured toward the door.

Dan stood up and stepped outside without saying another word. He got into his car, started it up, and drove away.

It was late. Dan found himself back on Interstate 80 heading back to Reno. The black sky seemed infinitely deep, full of diamond stars. There were few cars on the highway, which was good, because Dan was having trouble coordinating his movements. He kept in the far right lane and drove under the speed limit. He kept thinking of Ashley, and different memories of her flashed through his mind: her bowling, her cleaning tables, her laughing, her sitting across from him at Terri's restaurant or at the buffet in the casino... but the one image that kept returning to his mind the most was the image of her in the jungle walking beside the brujo, that smear of blood on her blouse, her arms tied behind her back. Dan decided that that image, for some reason, was her essence at this moment. He took another small sip of ayahuasca. He was driving through Sparks, still on Interstate 80, when he felt the liquid thought of turning north on state route 445. He took the exit, not knowing why. He looked up at the sky. It was no longer black, but blood red. He blinked his eyes hard twice. The sky returned to black but the light of the stars was too intense to look at. He had to hold his right hand over his eyes to shield them from the intense glare of the stars. He held onto the steering wheel with his left hand trying to stay on the road.

He got through the city of Sparks and was now heading north on 445 toward Spanish Springs. Here, there were only miles of desert separated by walled and gated real estate developments and occasional commercial centers. Dan slowed down. The ayahuasca was wearing off. Rational thoughts began to creep into his brain. What the fuck was he doing? Was he off his rocker? What if some cop pulled him over? He took another small sip of the brown liquid and kept driving. He thought of Ashley and immediately he felt a sound calling him to turn down a dirt road to his left. He turned off his headlights and turned down the road. The stars had stopped blinding him. In fact, he realized that it had started to cloud up and get darker. But there was still enough starlight where he could make out the dirt road. The terrain became hilly. He drove for another fifteen minutes, taking sips of ayahuasca every five minutes or so. Then he stopped his car, turned off the motor and got out. He was at the base of a large hill. The dirt road forked both left and right around the hill. Dan took the right fork and walked around the hill. Up ahead he could make out a small building. It looked abandoned. He took out his bottle of ayahuasca. There were just a few sips left. He took one, put the bottle back in his pocket, and started walking towards the building. It took him about ten minutes to cover the distance over the uneven desert terrain. As he got closer to the building, he slowed his pace down, trying to walk as softly as possible. It was an old shack, with a tin roof and tin walls. The tin was rattling in the breeze, but Dan could hear something on the other side of the building, some type of rhythmic sound. He finished the last sip of ayahuasca and put the empty bottle in his jacket pocket. He pulled his Ruger out of the holster and carefully crept around the building. There was a Toyota Corolla parked on the other side of the building, and next to it was a man digging a hole in the ground with a shovel. The man had his back to Dan.

Dan stepped closer, keeping his gun aimed on the man. He got up by the car, about fifteen feet from the man.

"You can stop right there, John."

John spun around. Dan kept his gun aimed at him, using both hands.

"Drop the shovel."

A look of panic came over John's face, but he dropped the shovel.

"Put your hands on the top of your head."

John put his hands on top of his head.

"Where's your gun?" Dan asked.

"I don't have a gun," John stammered.

Dan steadied his aim at the center of John's chest. "Don't fucking lie to me, John. Where's the gun?"

"In my right pocket."

Dan could feel his thoughts turning silvery as the last of the ayahuasca hit him. He made a quick cold glance at the Toyota. He could feel that Ashley was tied up, in the trunk. He had the impression she was beat pretty badly but was still alive. Dan looked over at John. He gave John the same quick cold look. John was going to kill her and bury her here. And this was not the first time he had killed. Dan could see into John's past. He had killed before. He liked killing. Dan looked into John's future. He was going to kill again. It made no sense because Dan knew that John was looking at a minimum prison sentence of twenty years, but Dan could see that John was going to kill again. Unless he was stopped. Stopped unless he was. Was unless stopped he. Dan's thoughts were turning to liquid.

Dan could hear Nate flying in erratic circles above him. He could see the brujo emerging from the grove of trees with a bundle of vines and leaves. He could smell the ayahuasca bubbling in the cauldron at his feet.

Dan aimed at the center of John's chest and pulled the trigger. The force of bullet knocked John backwards.

John grabbed his chest with his left hand and pushed himself up with his right. Blood started spurting out between his fingers of his left hand. He looked up at Dan in disbelief. Dan's second shot tore off the right side of John's head and he fell backwards, sprawling against the side of the hole he had been digging. He didn't move.

Dan put his Ruger back into his holster and walked over and looked at the lifeless body. Dan felt nothing inside, just an empty cold silence. He took his handkerchief from his back pocket and used it to reach into John's pocket and removed John's gun. He used the handkerchief to place the gun in John right hand and then lifted John's arm and aimed the gun into the desert and pulled the trigger. Then he let the gun fall into the dirt. He patted the outside of John's pants pockets looking for the car keys. He felt them in John's right pants pocket, along with something that felt like a cell phone. He used the handkerchief to reach in and remove both the cell phone and the car keys. He recognized the cell phone as the new one that he had helped Ashley pick out earlier that day. He stood up and thought about it for a minute. He could feel the ayahuasca leaving his system and being replaced by his detective brain. He took out his own cell phone and placed it on mute. He looked at both cell phones. There was just the barest of cell tower service, just one flickering bar of cell phone reception on each phone. Dan used his handkerchief to hit speed dial on Ashley's phone. His own phone started to vibrate. He answered his phone, and just stood there holding both phones for a full minute. Then he hit the "End Call" button on Ashley's phone and carefully put it back into John's pocket using the handkerchief. He then made sure his phone was disconnected from the call, and he put his phone and his handkerchief back into his pockets. He then grabbed John's car keys and went over to the car and opened the trunk.

There was Ashley, hogtied, with duct tape over her mouth, crammed into that tiny trunk. Even in the dim light, he could see that her face was beaten pretty badly. There was blood smeared all over her blouse. He wasn't sure if she was conscious or not but he started talking to her, saying "It's going to be alright Ashley, it's going to be alright" over and over. She managed to open one of her swollen eyes. Tears started rolling down her cheeks, mixing with the blood. Dan used his pocket knife to cut the ropes around her ankles, legs, wrists and arms. He slowly hoisted her out of the trunk of the car and carefully removed the duct tape from her mouth. When she could stand up, she wrapped her arms around him and just started sobbing and wailing. He just kept repeating "It's going to be alright." She held onto him like she never wanted to let go.

After a few minutes, she tried to talk.

"Where's John?"

"He's dead," Dan said.

She held him tighter.

"Look," Dan said, "we need to get you to a hospital. Can you walk?"

"I don't know."

She straightened up a bit, put some weight on her feet and winced.

"Well, I'm parked about a ten minute walk from here. You can wait here and I'll bring the car."

Ashley turned and looked over her shoulder at where John was laying sprawled on the ground by the hole. "No, don't leave me here."

"Well, then we have to walk."

"Okay, I'll walk."

Ashley hobbled and limped slowly, holding onto Dan, and they made their way over to where Dan's car was parked. He figured he was equidistant from the Northern Nevada Medical Center in Sparks and the West Hills Hospital in Reno, so he drove to Reno. On the way, he called 911 and was lucky to get patched through to the same desk sergeant he had talked to earlier that evening. He gave the desk sergeant the version of events that he thought would be the most plausible, described as best he could where John's body was, and explained that he was taking Ashley to West Hills Hospital. The desk sergeant told him he would notify Susan.

Before he got to the highway, he reached into his pocket and tossed the empty plastic bottle out of the window into the bushes.

At the hospital they were met by four or five police, including Susan. Susan looked weary from lack of sleep but happy that Ashley was safe. The police took one look at Susan and decided to let the emergency room doctor work on her first before they questioned her. She looked horrible. John had beaten her with his fists, fracturing an occipital bone around her eye, which broke the capillaries in her left eye, turning all the white of her eye a bright red. He had also broken her nose. Some type of ring he was wearing had open up gashes on her head, one of which needed stitches. Her face was covered with blood, but Dan learned later that the occipital bone fracture was a simple fracture and would heal on its own, and the doctor was able reset her broken nose. John had also beaten her body, but there were no broken bones and no apparent internal damage.

While the police waited for the doctor to finish treating Ashley, they took Dan's statement. He explained that, as he had told Susan earlier, he knew he couldn't just sit at home and wait, so he was driving around just hoping to spot John's car so he could call the police. He told them that he figured that John would have gotten out of town so that he wouldn't be spotted, and so it seemed most logical for Dan to drive around the outskirts of town. He told them he had driven around randomly for hours; that he had ended up north of Sparks; and that he was just about to give up and go home when John called him using Ashley's cell phone. He told them that Ashley had programmed his number into speed dial on her phone, a fact that Ashley later confirmed to them. He said that John told him he was holding Ashley hostage and would kill her unless Dan showed up and brought his ATM card and all his credit cards. Dan told them that he assumed that John didn't know he was a retired cop. Dan explained that he had assumed that John thought he was just Ashley's father or some old guy. Dan said that he would have called the police immediately after getting the call from John, but where he was driving he lost cell service and didn't get it back until after he had rescued Ashley. He said he had tried following John's directions but had gotten lost and had parked his car and was walking to the top of a hill to try and get oriented when he saw the building and walked up to it. He explained that John pulled a gun on him and bragged that he was going to kill both of them, and that then John had fired his gun at Dan but missed, and that that was when Dan pulled his gun and shot John in self-defense.

The police seemed satisfied with Dan's version of what happened. When the doctor finished treating Ashley, they let him visit with her for a few minutes. Her head was all bandaged up. There was a metal splint over her nose, and her left eye was swollen shut. Her face was puffy but she managed a smile when she saw him.

He patted her shoulder and said, "Well, I've seen you look better."

She started to smile more but then winced from the pain in her face. She tried to mumble something.

"No," Dan said, "don't talk. We'll have plenty of time to talk later. The doctors are going to keep you here for a few days. You just need to rest."

She reached over and took his hand and squeezed it hard.

"I'll come by and visit tomorrow," Dan said. Then he added, "You know, I remember being in the hospital as a kid and having my tonsils out. I got to eat all the ice cream I wanted. You be sure to ask them for ice cream, you hear?"

Ashley nodded her head and squeezed his hand again.

"Okay, kiddo. I'll see you tomorrow," Dan said and left the room.

As he walked out of the emergency room and into the lobby, he suddenly felt an overwhelming tiredness, almost dizzy. He put his arm up against the wall to brace himself. Susan came up to him and took his other arm for support.

"Are you alright, Mr. Landes?"

"Yeah, yeah, I'm okay... I'm just tired. I'm just too old for all this. I'm going to go home now, if you're done with me."

"Do you want us to drive you home, sir?"

"No, I'll be fine, thank you. If you have any more questions for me, you know where to find me."

"No, I think we have all we need."

Dan straightened up and walked slowly outside to his car. The fact is, he could have walked a bit faster, but he was tired, and besides, if thinking of him as an old man made Susan believe his story more, he was okay with walking slow.

Dan drove back to Sheila's Inn, parked in front of his room, and went inside. He could use another hot bath, he thought to himself, but he really was too damn tired. He poured a glass of whiskey and stretched out on the bed without taking his clothes off. He put the glass of whiskey on the side table by the bed intending to take a sip of it as soon as he adjusted the pillows, but as soon as his head touched the pillows, he felt himself starting to fall asleep. That's okay, he thought to himself, he was ready to sleep. Blessed sleep, he thought, that doth knit up the raveled sleeve of care....

He was back in the jungle. He looked up. The sun was coming up. Nate was gone from the sky. He looked over to the grove of trees. He knew the brujo was gone, too. He looked down at the cauldron by his feet. It was empty and the fire was out. There were a few pieces of cold burnt wood sticking out from under the pot. He looked around. He was alone. He started walking out of the jungle down the trail that he knew led to the village down in the valley.

As he walked he was thinking, "This is the real reality." The world of Reno and that girl Ashley was just a dream, a long strange dream that had flowed through his head like liquid. The walk to the village would take two hours. From there, he could catch a local bus to Cerro Punta. He might have to spend the night in Cerro Punta, but he knew that within a day, and two or three bus rides more, he could be back in Villa Rosario.

Chapter 15

The Dan that woke up the next morning was a different Dan that the man who had moved to Reno five months earlier. The man who woke up that morning opened his eyes and looked around his motel room, at the old cracked and worn walls. This man knew he would be leaving this place soon. He looked at the back of his hands. They looked normal, but they also looked old, cracked and worn as well. He examined the faded tattoo on his left hand… three small dots on the fleshy fold of skin between his thumb and his first finger. An old tattoo from a life long ago. Well, that tattoo was old, but ayahuasca had tattooed his soul anew last night. Ayahuasca had finally chosen him, given him a gift, and now he was indebted. That old question that he had asked the brujo so many decades ago came back to him: Un devoto o un esclavo?—a devotee or a slave? Well, now Dan had the answer. He was indebted to ayahuasca. He may not be a slave but he was an indentured servant, so what was the difference? He knew where he had to go to work off the debt—he had to go back to Panama. Yes, he would go back to Panama. He would renew his friendship with don Fernando. He would do little projects with don Fernando again. And he would drink ayahuasca again. Those were just facts. But first, he would stay in Reno long enough to make sure Ashley was okay. Two, maybe three months… but then he would go back to Villa Rosario. But for now, he would play his part… he would continue the role that he had been creating for all these decades… he knew how the stage of his life was set… where his points were marked… where he had to stand… how the stage was blocked… his entrance cues… he knew his lines. He could play the old retired detective two or three months more. It would be easy. For example, now he would simply get up and make some coffee and start his morning....

Over the next couple of days, as the police put together the various pieces of evidence, everything corroborated Dan's story: Ashley told the police how John had told her that he had followed her to the casino and seen her walk with Dan to the police station; the police found Ashley's cell phone in John's pocket; Ashley confirmed that he had taken it from her; they found Dan's number in Ashley's speed dial; the cell phone records showed that a call had been placed to Dan's phone number; John's gun had been fired one time and there were visible powder marks on his hand. Plus there was the obvious grave that John had been digging and the vicious beating he had given Ashley. The final clincher was when they sent John's fingerprints to the FBI's database and discovered that he had served three years in a New Jersey prison for manslaughter and was a person of interest in another unsolved murder in Oklahoma.

At one point during a follow-up meeting, Susan chided Dan for not driving back to Reno into good cell reception once he had gotten John's call and calling the police rather than driving to meet John. But she had to acknowledge that if he had done that, then Ashley probably would have been killed. Dan told her he should have done that, and he would have done that, but that he was so exhausted with worry that night that he wasn't thinking straight. Dan wasn't totally sure she believed everything about his story, but, like every cop he ever had known, he knew that she would be willing to overlook minor inconsistencies when the overall result was good. John was a bad guy. John was dead. Dan was an old ex-cop who happened to be there and had to shoot John in self-defense. Case closed. End of story.

Ashley's face healed slowly. After six weeks, the only physical evidence of the beating she had taken was a small scar above her left eye, and a small bump on her nose that Dan thought was rather attractive. It took her awhile to get back into bowling form, as she had a number of bruises and contusions on her legs and arms, but after a few weeks of practice she looked as graceful as ever.

Marcie made a full recovery as well. John's blow with the crowbar had fractured her skull, and she actually had to remain in the hospital twice as long as Ashley, but eventually she was fine.

Dan still thought about that murder in La Chorrera, but not in the same way as before. He thought about it in the same light that he thought about his murdering John, and in the same way he thought of Nate breaking his legs. The choices that we make lead unalterably to the outcomes we inherit. Nate's foolish bribe of the brujo into giving him ayahuasca that he wasn't ready to drink led directly to his sprouting wings he couldn't control and crashing to the ground. Ashley's foolish decision to give John another chance put her directly in harm's way. John's life of deceit and rage led to his own violent death in the Nevada desert. And Dan's decision to drink ayahuasca again led directly to his murdering John. It's as if the freedom of choice we have is all at the beginning of events, and from that point on, the die is cast. Les jeux sont fait, as Sartre said.... Alea iacta est, as Julius Caesar said, crossing the Rubicon River.... La suerte está echada, as don Fernando had once told him about the murder of that suspect in La Chorrera. The die is cast.

Dan chose to drink ayahuasca because he had chosen to try and find Ashley; and he chose to search for her because he had chosen to fall in love with her; and he chose to fall in love with her because he had chosen to come to Reno and open himself up to being healed; and he chose to come back to the states to be healed because he had chosen to help his friend don Fernando catch a murder suspect in La Chorrera; and the murder of that suspect had disrupted ten years of choices and assumptions he had made about Panamanian culture; but nonetheless, he had chosen to live in Panama because he did love that culture—a culture he was exposed to when he was just out of college and chose to accompany Nate to Panama to seek ayahuasca…. Life is just an endless connection of free choices that lead to inevitable unexpected consequence which then lead to more free choices and more inevitable unexpected consequences. Only in retrospect do we see the immutable and unalterable link between our choices and our fates. Our "free choices" are not that free. We see that looking backwards. It's only rarely that we get a prospective glimpse of the fate that awaits us. Sometimes it comes to us in a quick cold intuitive glance to the future... or in dreams... or sometimes, in a smoky pungent intoxicant that turns our rational thoughts to liquid and lets an image appear of something that does not exist yet, and yet... there it is.

The future is as cyclical as our past. Dan had spent most of his adult life traveling back and forth to Panama as often as he could afford to, and finally settling there. And soon he would return there. He had no choice about that. And he knew he would see don Fernando again and that he would be happy to see him again. Dan had already forgiven him, just as he had already forgiven himself. Don Fernando had no choice in arranging the murder of that man in the jail cell in La Chorrera, just has Dan had no choice in murdering John. Of course, Dan knew that a jury could find him accountable if they knew the true facts of John's murder, but no one would ever know the true facts, and in Dan's heart, he knew that was the way it should be. He also knew that both murders still were completely contrary to his personal belief system of how justice should work, but he now accepted how puny, arbitrary, and fragile that belief system was. A few alkaloid molecules can rip our rational minds to shreds, and a simple ancient cultural tradition can rip our sense of justice to shreds. Either way, Dan simply had to learn to manage it. He would build iron fences where he had to, and he would build gates where he could. He would go back to square one, and try to understand the real Panamanian culture, and he would go back and try to repay his debt to ayahuasca.

Of course, during the three months while Ashley was healing, he did give a great deal of thought to his relationship with her. After all, his decision to drink ayahuasca was due to his feelings for her. And he did love her—he knew that. How could he not? She was young and lithe and smart and sweet. But he was old and worn out, like a piece of flint. He loved her, but the age difference was vast, and the difference in worldviews vaster. In the months after the beating, it would have been easy to mistake her gratitude to him for love. Dan knew she cared, but he could see that the feelings she felt sprung from gratitude and trust, not from the kind of mature love that could survive the age difference over time. He had taken enough quick cold glimpses into her future to see that she would eventually partner with a man who would be closer to her age, a better man than he was. Or maybe it would be a woman—it made no difference, because Dan could see that she was one of those people who stood a chance at finding happiness, who still believed in love, and he wasn't going to be the one to ruin her chances by taking advantage of her gratitude, exploiting her trust, and turning their relationship into something sexual that would only leave her feeling used and bitter. He recognized that the condition that he had decided on months ago—that he would only sleep with her if she initiated it—was still the best litmus test of their relationship. And while they spent a lot of time together after she was released from the hospital—dinners, lunches, hikes, bowling, even dancing—and while they hugged and were cozy, she never initiated sex or gave him those classic permissions that women give when they want men to initiate sex. He knew his decision was the right one. She was starting to talk a lot about going back to school, pursuing that Master's degree she always wanted, and Dan was very supportive of that idea. Besides, he had already decided to return to Panama.

He was trying to explain his need to return to Panama to her one night, over dinner, down at Terri's restaurant. He had purchased his plane ticket and he was set to leave in ten days.

"It's hard to explain," Dan was saying, "because it's not an experience that everyone has… but… have you ever visited a place, like, gone on vacation to a place that just feels magical? That just has a certain vibration to it that makes you feel at home?   It's like meeting someone you click with immediately, or finding an apartment to rent that is just perfect, and you know immediately that it's perfect. Well, Panama's like that to me. That's not to say it's perfect—it's not perfect. Nothing happens fast there and nothing is easy, but it has this vibration, this *feel* that I can't describe… I just feel at home there. It *is* my home, really, as close to a home as anywhere I've lived… so I want to go back."

"I think I understand," Ashley said. "It does sound wonderful. But I'm really going to miss you, Dan." She reached over and took his hand.

"I'm going to miss you too, Ashley," he said, squeezing her hand, "but there's email, and Skype, and hard-to-believe but Panama has a mail service too, although I don't know if anyone actually writes real letters anymore."

"True," she said, "but even Skype is not the same as sitting across the table from you and just being able to talk."

Dan nodded.

"I'm *really* going to miss you," she said again, and squeezed his hand harder. "Maybe…" she paused, "maybe I could come visit you?" she asked.

"Of course you can," Dan said, although he had never seen that possibility in his glimpses into her future, but he certainly was not opposed to it. "I'd love to show you around my world."

She smiled and said, "I would really like that."

Dan thought for a minute. He didn't see it happening, didn't have any images of him showing her around Panama, didn't have any intuition about it one way or another, but who knew? Maybe, he thought, this was one of those "free choice" moments that creates certain outcomes, so he said, "I tell you what. If you get admitted into graduate school somewhere, some MSW program, and as a reward, if you still want to come visit, I'll pay for your airline ticket. How 'bout dem apples?"

"Really?!!" she exclaimed. "That would be so great!"

Dan didn't know what the outcome of that offer would be. The application process, he knew, took time. Assuming she found the right school to apply to, it would be at least seven to eight months before she'd know their decision. That was alright, he thought. It would give both of them time. They both needed time—she needed time to get over that horrible experience with John and to take charge of her own life, time to grow up a little bit and be responsible; and he needed time to settle back down in Panama and start life new again, and to also learn some new responsibilities. Yes, seven or eight months would be a useful amount of time. Time... that doth knit up the raveled sleeve of care.

She interrupted his reverie. "What are you thinking about?" she asked. "You had that faraway look in your eyes again, like you were in another world."

He looked at her and smiled.

"Yeah... I was."

-FIN-

ABOUT THE AUTHOR

Over the past 30 years, Robert Rahula has published dozens books of prose and poetry in Spain and in the United States. While he remains relatively undiscovered in the United States, he is revered in Spain as the founder of the "portilla" style of popular Spanish poetry: non-metered fluid verse that deals with love, loss, bisexuality, separateness, and growing older.

Robert was born in Spain to an American father and Spanish mother, but grew up in Virginia on the farm of his paternal grandparents. He returned to Menorca, Spain, in the 1960s to pursue his writing career. These days he travels in Europe, Central and South America for several months a year, giving readings and lectures, and spends the rest of his time writing, dividing his time between Spain and the United States.

All of Robert's English books are still in print or available as ebooks, including his groundbreaking erotic novel *Messieurs*; his second English novel *Panamaniac;* his erotic murder mystery *Island of Misfits*; his surreal novel *Day Another Paradise In;* his acclaimed supernatural novel *One Last Fling;* his "sexistential" novel *Conversations in a Belgian Bar;* as well as his "Dan Landes Mystery" novels: *Bathhouse Stories, All the Yage in Reno, Exigent Circumstances, and Uninvited Guest.*

Eight volumes of Robert's English poetry are also available: *Trigger Points; Inside the Locked Heart; Camino; Migration; I Sing the Body Politic; Wonderland; From Whose Bourn; Expat Poems; plus* an anthology of his English poems and short stories, *Half-Life;* and a collection of his most famous Spanish poems, *Poemas Españoles.* Other poems, along with his blog on writing and his tour itinerary, appear on his Facebook page and on his website robertrahula.com.